P9-BXZ-908

FIRST TIME IN PAPERBACK!

RONICKY DOONE

MAX BRAND

**Author of Millions of Books in Print!
"Brand's Westerns are good reading and crammed
with adventure!"
—*Chicago Tribune***

**A writer of legendary genius, Max Brand has
brought to his Westerns the raw frontier action and
historical authenticity that have earned him the title
of world's most celebrated Western writer.**

In *Ronicky Doone*, the Old West is not a place for a four-
flushing backshooter or a cowardly claim jumper. But the
wild land is just the place for a fearless roustabout like
Ronicky Doone. The trouble is, anywhere Doone goes,
trouble is sure to follow. As luck has it, though, Ronicky
Doone is one ornery cayuse who can outshoot any worthless
desperado who takes aim on his hide.

Other *Leisure Books* by Max Brand:
BLACKIE AND RED
THE WHISPERING OUTLAW
THE SHADOW OF SILVER TIP
THE TRAP AT COMANCHE BEND
THE MOUNTAIN FUGITIVE

MAX BRAND

RONICKY DOONE

LEISURE BOOKS  NEW YORK CITY

RONICKY
DOONE

Chapter One

A Horse in Need

He came into the town as a solid, swiftly moving dust cloud. The wind from behind had kept the dust moving forward at a pace just equal to the gallop of his horse. Not until he had brought his mount to a halt in front of the hotel and swung down to the ground did either he or his horse become distinctly visible. Then it was seen that the animal was in the last stages of exhaustion, with dull eyes and hanging head and forelegs braced widely apart, while the sweat dripped steadily from his flanks into the white dust on the street. Plainly he had been pushed to the last limit of his strength.

The rider was almost as far spent as his mount, for he went up the steps of the hotel with his shoulders sagging with weariness, a wide-shouldered, gaunt-ribbed man. Thick layers of dust had turned his red kerchief and his blue shirt to a common gray. Dust, too, made a mask of his face, and through that mask the eyes peered out, surrounded by pink skin. Even at its best the long, solemn face could never have been called handsome. But, on this particular day, he seemed a haunted man, or one fleeing from an inescapable danger.

The two loungers at the door of the hotel instinctively stepped aside and made room for him to pass, but apparently he had no desire to enter the building. Suddenly he became doubly imposing, as he stood on the veranda and stared up and down at the idlers. Certainly his throat must be thick and hot with dust, but an overmastering purpose made him oblivious of thirst.

"Gents," he said huskily, while a gust of wind fanned a cloud of dust from his clothes, "is there anybody in this town can gimme a hoss to get to Stillwater, inside three hours' riding?"

He waited a moment, his hungry eyes traveling eagerly from face to face. Naturally the oldest man spoke first, since this was a matter of life and death.

"Any hoss in town can get you there in that time, if you know the short way across the mountain."

"How do you take it? That's the way for me."

But the old fellow shook his head and smiled in pity. "Not if you ain't rode it before. I used to go that way when I was a kid, but nowadays nobody rides that way except Doone. That trail is as tricky as the ways of a coyote; you'd sure get lost without a guide."

The stranger turned and followed the gesture of the speaker. The mountain rose from the very verge of the town, a ragged mass of sand and rock, with miserable sagebrush clinging here and there, as dull and uninteresting as the dust itself. Then he lowered the hand from beneath which he had peered and faced about with a sigh. "I guess it ain't much good trying that way. But I got to get to Stillwater inside of three hours."

"They's one hoss in town can get you there," said the old man. "But you can't get that hoss today."

The stranger groaned. "Then I'll make another hoss stretch out and do."

"Can't be done. Doone's hoss is a marvel. Nothing else about here can touch him, and he's the only one that can make the trip around the mountain, inside of three hours. You'd kill another hoss trying to do it, what with your weight."

The stranger groaned again and struck his knuckles against his forehead. "But why can't I get the hoss? Is Doone out of town with it?"

"The hoss ain't out of town, but Doone is."

The traveler clenched his fists. This delay and waste of priceless time was maddening him. "Gents," he called desperately, "I got to get to Martindale today. It's more than life or death to me. Where's Doone's hoss?"

"Right across the road," said the old man who had spoken first. "Over yonder in the corral—the bay."

The traveler turned and saw, beyond the road, a beautiful mare, not very tall, but a mare whose every inch of her fifteen three proclaimed strength and speed. At that moment she raised her head and looked across to him, and the heart of the rider jumped into his throat. The very sight of her was an omen of victory, and he made a long stride in her direction, but two men came before him. The old fellow jumped from the chair and tapped his arm.

"You ain't going to take the bay without getting leave from Doone?"

"Gents, I got to," said the stranger. "Listen! My name's Gregg, Bill Gregg. Up in my country they know I'm straight; down here you ain't heard of me. I ain't going to keep that hoss, and I'll pay a hundred dollars for the use of her for one day. I'll bring or send her back safe and sound, tomorrow. Here's the money. One of you gents, that's a friend of Doone, take it for him."

Not a hand was stretched out; every head shook in negation.

"I'm too fond of the little life that's left to me," said the old fellow. "I won't rent out that hoss for him. Why, he loves that mare like she was his sister. He'd fight like a flash rather than see another man ride her."

But Bill Gregg had his eyes on the bay, and the sight of her was stealing his reason. He knew, as well as he knew that he was a man, that, once in the saddle on her, he would be sure to win. Nothing could stop him. And straight through the restraining circle he broke with a groan of anxiety.

Only the old man who had been the spokesman called after him: "Gregg, don't be a fool. Maybe you don't recognize the name of Doone, but the whole name is Ronicky Doone. Does that mean anything to you?"

Into the back of Gregg's mind came several faint memories, but they were obscure and uncertain. "Blast your Ronicky Doone!" he replied. "I got to have that hoss, and, if none of you'll take money for her rent, I'll take her free and pay her rent when I come through this way tomorrow, maybe. S'long!"

While he spoke he had been undoing the cinches of his own horse. Now he whipped the saddle and bridle off, shouted to the hotel keeper brief instructions for the care of the weary animal and ran across the road with the saddle on his arm.

In the corral he had no difficulty with the mare. She came straight to him in spite of all the flopping trappings. With prickly ears and eyes lighted with kindly curiosity she looked the dusty fellow over.

He slipped the bridle over her head. When he swung the saddle over her back she merely turned her head and carelessly watched it fall. And when he drew up the cinches hard, she only stamped in mock anger. The moment he was in the saddle she tossed her head eagerly, ready to be off.

He looked across the street to the veranda of the hotel, as he passed through the gate of the corral. The men were standing in a long and awe-stricken line, their eyes wide, their mouths agape. Whoever Ronicky Doone might be, he was certainly a man who had won the respect of this town. The men on the veranda looked at Bill Gregg as though he were already a ghost. He waved his hand defiantly at them and the mare, at a word from him, sprang into a long-striding gallop that whirled them rapidly down the street and out of the village.

The bay mare carried him with amazing speed over the ground. They rounded the base of the big mountain, and, glancing up at the ragged canyons which chopped the face of the peak, he was glad that he had not attempted that short cut. If Ronicky Doone could make that trail he was a skillful horseman.

Bill Gregg swung up over the left shoulder of the mountain and found himself looking down on the wide plain which held Stillwater. The air was crystal-clear and dry; the shoulder of the mountain was high above it; Gregg saw a breathless stretch of the cattle country at one sweep of his eyes.

Stillwater was still a long way off, and far away across the plain he saw a tiny moving dot that grew slowly. It was the train heading for Stillwater, and that train he must beat to the station. For a moment his heart stood still; then he saw that the train was distant indeed, and, by the slightest use of the mare's speed, he would be able to reach the town, two or three minutes ahead of it.

But, just as he was beginning to exult in the victory, after all the hard riding of the past three days, the mare tossed up her head and shortened her stride. The heart of Gregg stopped, and he went cold. It was not only the fear that his journey might be ruined, but the fear that something had happened to this magnificent creature beneath him. He swung to the side in the saddle and watched her gallop. Certain she went laboring, very much as though she were trying to run against a mighty pull on the reins.

He looked at her head. It was thrown high, with pricking ears. Perhaps she was frightened by some foolish thing near the road. He touched her with the spurs, and she increased her pace to the old length and ease of stride; but, just as he had begun to be reassured, her step shortened and fell to laboring again, and this time she threw her head higher than before. It was amazing to Bill Gregg; and then it seemed to him that he heard a faint, far whistling, floating down from high above his head.

Again that thin, long-drawn sound, and this time, glancing over his right shoulder, he saw a horseman plunging down the slope of the mountain. He knew instantly that it was Ronicky Doone. The man had come to recapture his horse and had taken the short cut across the mountain to come up with her. Just by a fraction of a minute Doone would be too late, for, by the time he came down onto the trail, the bay would be well ahead, and certainly no horse lived in those mountains capable of overtaking her when she felt like running. Gregg touched her again with the spurs, but this time she reared straight up and, whirling to the side, faced steadily toward her onrushing master.

Chapter Two

Friendly Enemies

Again and again Gregg spurred the bay cruelly.

She winced from the pain and snorted, but, apparently having not the slightest knowledge of bucking, she could only shake her head and send a ringing whinny of appeal up the slope of the mountain, toward the approaching rider.

In spite of the approaching danger, in spite of this delay which was ruining his chances of getting to Stillwater before the train, Bill Gregg watched in marvel and delight the horsemanship of the stranger. Ronicky Doone, if this were he, was certainly the prince of all wild riders.

Even as the mare stopped in answer to the signal of her owner, Ronicky Doone sent his mount over the edge of a veritable cliff, flung him back on his haunches and slid down the gravelly slope, careening from side to side. With a rush of pebbles about him and a dust cloud whirling after, Ronicky Doone broke out into the road ahead of the mare, and she whinnied softly again to greet him.

Bill Gregg found himself looking not into the savage face of such a gunfighter as he had been led to expect, but a handsome fellow, several years younger than he, a high-headed, straight-eyed, buoyant type. In his seat in the saddle, in the poise of his head and the play of his hand on the reins Bill Gregg recognized a boundless nervous force. There was nothing ponderous about Ronicky Doone. Indeed he was not more than middle size, but, as he reined his horse in the middle of the road and looked with flashing eyes at Bill Gregg, he appeared very large indeed.

Gregg was used to fighting or paying his way, or doing both at the same time, as occasion offered. He decided that this was certainly an occasion for much money and few words.

"You're Doone, I guess," he said, "and you know that I've played a pretty bad trick on you, taking your hoss this way. But I wanted to pay for it, Doone, and I'll pay now. I've got to get to Stillwater before that train. Look at her! I haven't hurt her any. Her wind isn't touched. She's pretty wet, but sweat never hurt nothing on four feet, eh?"

"I dunno," returned Ronicky Doone. "I'd as soon run off with a man's wife as his hoss."

"Partner," said Bill Gregg desperately, "I have to get there!"

"Then get there on your own feet, not the feet of another gent's hoss."

Gregg controlled his rising anger. Beyond him the train was looming larger and larger in the plain, and Stillwater seemed more and more distant. He writhed in the saddle.

"I tell you I'll pay—I'll pay the whole value of the hoss, if you want."

He was about to say more when he saw the eyes of Ronicky Doone widen and fix.

"Look," said the other suddenly, "you've been cutting her up with the spurs!"

Gregg glanced down to the flank of the bay to discover that he had used the spurs more recklessly than he thought. A sharp rowel had picked through the skin, and, though it was probably only a slight wound indeed, it had brought a smear of red to the surface.

Ronicky Doone trembled with anger.

"Confound you!" he said furiously. "Any fool would have known that you didn't need a spur on that hoss! What part d'you come from where they teach you to kill a hoss when you ride it? Can you tell me that?"

"I'll tell you after I get to Stillwater."

"I'll see you hung before I see you in Stillwater."

"You've talked too much, Doone," Gregg said huskily.

"I've just begun," said Doone.

"Then take this and shut up," exclaimed Bill Gregg.

Ordinarily he was the straightest and the squarest man in the world in a fight. But a sudden anger had flared up in him. He had an impulse to kill; to get rid of this obstacle between him and everything he wanted most in life. Without more warning than that he snatched out his revolver and fired point blank at Ronicky Doone. Certainly all the approaches to a fight had been made, and Doone might have been expecting the attack. At any rate, as the gun shot out of Gregg's holster, the other swung himself sidewise in his own saddle and, snapping out his revolver, fired from the hip.

That swerve to the side saved him, doubtless, from the shot of Gregg; his own bullet plowed cleanly through the thigh of the other rider. The whole leg of Gregg went numb, and he found himself slumping helplessly to one side. He dropped his gun, and he had to cling with both hands to lower himself out of the saddle. Now he sat in the dust of the trail and stared stupidly, not at his conqueror, but at the train that was flashing into the little town of Stillwater, just below them.

He hardly heeded Ronicky Doone, as the latter started forward with an oath, knelt beside him and examined the wound. "It's clean," Doone said, as he started ripping up his undershirt to make bandages. "I'll have you fixed so you can be gotten into Stillwater."

He began to work rapidly, twisting the clothes around Gregg's thigh, which he had first laid bare by some dexterous use of a hunting knife.

Then Gregg turned his eyes to those of Doone. The train had pulled out of Stillwater. The sound of the coughing of the engine, as it started up, came faintly to them after a moment.

"Of all the darned fools!" said the two men in one voice.

And then they grinned at each other. Certainly it was not the first fight or the first wound for either of them.

"I'm sorry," they began again, speaking together in chorus.

"Matter of fact," said Ronicky Doone, "that bay means a pile to me. When I seen the red on her side—"

"Can't be more than a chance prick."

"I know," said Ronicky, "but I didn't stop to think."

"And I should of give you fair warning before I went for the gat."

"Look here," said Ronicky, "you talk like a straight sort of a gent to me."

"And you thought I was a cross between a hoss thief and a gunfighter?"

"I dunno what I thought, except that I wanted the mare back. Stranger, I'm no end sorry this has happened. Maybe you'd lemme know why you was in such a hurry to get to Stillwater. If they's any trouble coming down the road behind you, maybe I can help take care of it for you." And he smiled coldly and significantly at Bill Gregg.

The latter eyed with some wonder the man who had just shot him down and was now offering to fight for his safety. "Nothing like that," said Bill. "I was going to Stillwater to meet a girl."

"As much of a rush as all that to see a girl?"

"On that train."

Ronicky Doone whistled softly. "And I messed it up! But why didn't you tell me what you wanted?"

"I didn't have a chance. Besides I could not waste time in talking and explaining to everybody along the road."

"Sure you couldn't, but the girl'll forgive you when she finds out what happened."

"No, she won't, because she'll never find out."

"Eh?"

"I don't know where she is."

"Riding all that way just to see a girl—"

"It's a long story, partner, and this leg is beginning to act up. Tell you the best thing would be for you to jump on your mare and jog into Stillwater for a buckboard and then come back and get me. What d'you say?"

Twenty minutes after Ronicky Doone had swung into the saddle and raced down the road, the buckboard arrived and the wounded man was helped on to a pile of blankets in the body of the wagon.

The shooting, of course, was explained by the inevitable gun accident. Ronicky Doone happened to be passing along that way and saw Bill Gregg looking over his revolver as he rode along. At that moment the gun exploded and—

The two men who had come out in the buck-board listened to the tale with expressionless faces. As a matter of fact they had already heard in Stillwater that no less a person than Ronicky Doone was on his way toward that village in pursuit of a man who had ridden off on the famous bay mare, Lou. But they accepted Ronicky's bland version of the accident with perfect calm and with many expressions of sympathy. They would have other things to say after they had deposited the wounded man in Stillwater.

The trip in was a painful one for Bill Gregg. For one thing the exhaustion of the long three days' trip was now causing a wave of weariness to sweep over him. The numbness, which had come through the leg immediately after the shooting, was now replaced by a steady and continued aching. And more than all he was unnerved by the sense of utter failure, utter loss. Never in his life had he fought so bitterly and steadily for a thing, and yet he had lost at the very verge of success.

Chapter Three

At Stillwater

The true story was, of course, known almost at once, but, since Ronicky Doone swore that he would tackle the first man who accused him of having shot down Bill Gregg, the talk was confined to whispers. In the meantime Stillwater rejoiced in its possession of Ronicky Doone. Beyond one limited section of the mountain desert he was not as yet known, but he had one of those personalities which are called electric. Whatever he did seemed greater because he, Ronicky Doone, had done it.

Not that he had done a great many things as yet. But there was a peculiar feeling in the air that Ronicky Doone was capable of great and strange performances. Men older than he were willing to accept him as their leader; men younger than he idolized him.

Ronicky Doone, then, the admired of all beholders, is leaning in the doorway of Stillwater's second and best hotel. His bandanna today is a terrific yellow, set off with crimson half-moon and stars strewn liberally on it. His shirt is merely white, but it is given some significance by having nearly half of a red silk handkerchief falling out of the breast pocket. His sombrero is one of those works of art which Mexican families pass from father to son, only his was new and had not yet received that limp effect of age. And, like the gaudiest Mexican head piece, the band of this sombrero was of purest gold, beaten into the forms of various saints. Ronicky Doone knew nothing at all about saints, but he approved very much of the animation of the martyrdom scenes and felt reasonably sure that his hatband could not be improved upon in the entire length and breadth of Stillwater, and the young men of the town agreed with him, to say nothing of the girls.

They also admired his riding gloves which, a strange affectation in a country of buckskin, were always the softest and the smoothest and the most comfortable kid that could be obtained.

Truth to tell, he did not handle a rope. He could not tell the noose end of a lariat from the straight end, hardly. Neither did Ronicky Doone know the slightest thing about barbed wire, except how to cut it when he wished to ride through. Let us look closely at the hands themselves, as Ronicky stands in the door of the hotel and stares at the people walking by. For he has taken off his gloves and he now rolls a cigarette.

They are very long hands. The fingers are extremely slender and tapering. The wrists are round and almost as innocent of sinews as the wrists of a woman, save when he grips something, and then how they stand out. But, most remarkable of all, the skin of the palms of those hands is amazingly soft. It is truly as soft as the skin of the hand of a girl.

There were some who shook their heads when they saw those hands. There were some who inferred that Ronicky Doone was little better than a scapegrace, and that, in reality, he had never done a better or more useful thing than handle cards and swing a revolver. In both of which arts it was admitted that he was incredibly dexterous. As a matter of fact, since there was no estate from which he drew an income, and since he had never been known in the entire history of his young life to do a single stroke of productive work of any kind, the bitter truth was that Ronicky Doone was no better and no worse than a common gambler.

Indeed, if to play a game of chance is to commit a sin, Ronicky Doone was a very great sinner. Yet it should be remarked that he lacked the fine art of taking the money of other less clever fellows when they were intoxicated, and he also lacked the fine hardness of mind which enables many gamblers to enjoy taking the last cent from an opponent. Also, though he knew the entire list of tricks in the repertoire of a crooked gambler, he had never been known to employ tricking. He trusted in a calm head, a quick judgment, an ability to read character. And, though he occasionally met with crooked professionals who were wolves in the guise of sheep, no one had ever been known to play more than one crooked trick at cards when playing against Ronicky Doone. So, on the whole, he made a very good living.

What he had he gave or threw away in wild spending or loaned to friends, of whom he had a vast number. All of which goes to explain the soft hands of Ronicky Doone and his nervous, swift-moving fingers, as he stood at the door of the hotel. For he who plays long with cards or dice begins to have a special sense developed in the tips of his fingers, so that they seem to be independent intelligences.

He crossed his feet. His boots were the finest leather, bench-made by the best of bootmakers, and they fitted the high-arched instep with the elastic smoothness of gloves. The man of the mountain desert dresses the extremities and cares not at all for the mid sections. The moment Doone was off his horse those boots had to be dressed and rubbed and polished to softness and brightness before this luxurious gambler would walk about town. From the heels of the boots extended a long pair of spurs—surely a very great vanity, for never in her life had his beautiful mare, Lou, needed even the touch of a spur.

But Ronicky Doone could not give up this touch of luxury. The spurs were plated heavily with gold, and they swept up and out in a long, exquisite curve, the hub of the rowel set with diamonds.

In a word Ronicky Doone was a dandy, but he had this peculiarity, that he seemed to dress to please himself rather than the rest of the world. His glances never roved about taking account of the admiration of others. As he leaned there in the door of the hotel he was the type of the young, happy, genuine and carefree fellow, whose mind is no heavier with a thousand dollars or a thousand cents in his pocket.

Suddenly he started from his lounging place, caught his hat more firmly over his eyes, threw away his unlighted cigarette and hurried across the veranda of the hotel. Had he seen an enemy to chastise, or an old friend to greet, or a pretty girl? No, it was only old Jud Harding, the blacksmith, whose hand had lost its strength, but who still worked iron as others mold putty, simply because he had the genius for his craft. He was staggering now under a load of boards which he had shouldered to carry to his shop. In a moment that load was shifted to the shoulder of Ronicky Doone, and they went on down the street, laughing and talking together until the load was dropped on the floor of Harding's shop.

"And how's the sick feller coming?" asked Harding.

"Coming fine," answered Ronicky. "Couple of days and I'll have him out for a little exercise. Lucky thing it was a clean wound and didn't nick the bone. Soon as it's healed over he'll never know he was plugged."

Harding considered his young friend with twinkling eyes. "Queer thing to me," he said, "is how you and this gent Gregg have hit it off so well together. Might almost say it was like you'd shot Gregg and now was trying to make up for it. But, of course, that ain't the truth."

"Of course not," said Ronicky gravely and met the eye of Harding without faltering.

"Another queer thing," went on the cunning old smith. "He was fooling with that gun while he was in the saddle, which just means that the muzzle must of been pretty close to his skin. But there wasn't any sign of a powder burn, the doc says."

"But his trousers was pretty bad burned, I guess," said Ronicky.

"H-m," said the blacksmith, "that's the first time I've heard about it." He went on more seriously: "I got something to tell you, Ronicky. Ever hear the story about the gent that took pity on the snake that was stiff with cold and brought the snake in to warm him up beside the fire? The minute the snake come to life he sunk his fangs in the gent that had saved him."

"Meaning," said Ronicky, "that, because I've done a good turn for Gregg, I'd better look out for him?"

"Meaning nothing," said Harding, "except that the reason the snake bit the gent was because he'd had a stone heaved at him by the same man one day and hadn't forgot it."

But Ronicky Doone merely laughed and turned back toward the hotel.

Chapter Four

His Victim's Trouble

Yet he could not help pondering on the words of old Harding. Bill Gregg had been a strange patient. He had never repeated his first offer to tell his story. He remained sullen and silent, with his brooding eyes fixed on the blank wall before him, and nothing could permanently cheer him. Some inward gloom seemed to possess the man.

The first day after the shooting he had insisted on scrawling a painfully written letter, while Ronicky propped a writing board in front of him, as he lay flat on his back in the bed, but that was his only act. Thereafter he remained silent and brooding. Perhaps it was hatred for Ronicky that was growing in him, as the sense of disappointment increased, for Ronicky, after all, had kept him from reaching that girl when the train passed through Stillwater. Perhaps, for all Ronicky knew, his bullet had ruined the happiness of two lives. He shrugged that disagreeable thought away, and, reaching the hotel, he went straight up to the room of the sick man.

"Bill," he said gently, "have you been spending all your time hating me? Is that what keeps you thin and glum? Is it because you sit here all day blaming me for all the things that have happened to you?"

The dark flush and the uneasy flicker of Gregg's glance gave a sufficient answer. Ronicky Doone sighed and shook his head, but not in anger.

"You don't have to talk," he said. "I see that I'm right. And I don't blame you, Bill, because, maybe, I've spoiled things pretty generally for you."

At first the silence of Bill Gregg admitted that he felt the same way about the matter, yet he finally said aloud: "I don't blame you. Maybe you thought I was a hoss thief. But the thing is done, Ronicky, and it won't never be undone!"

"Gregg," said Ronicky, "d'you know what you're going to do now?"

"I dunno."

"You're going to sit there and roll a cigarette and tell me the whole yarn. You ain't through with this little chase. Not if I have to drag you along with me. But first just figure that I'm your older brother or something like that and get rid of the whole yarn. Got to have the ore specimens before you can assay 'em. Besides, it'll help you a pile to get the poison out of your system. If you feel like cussing me hearty when the time comes go ahead and cuss, but I got to hear that story."

"Maybe it would help," said Gregg, "but it's a fool story to tell."

"Leave that to me to say whether it's a fool story or not. You start the talking."

Gregg shifted himself to a more comfortable position, as is the immemorial custom of story tellers, and his glance misted a little with the flood of recollections.

"Started along back about a year ago," he said. "I was up to the Sullivan Mountains working a claim. There wasn't much to it, just enough to keep me going sort of comfortable. I pegged away at it pretty steady, leading a lonely life and hoping every day that I'd cut my way down to a good lead. Well, the fine ore never showed up.

"Meantime I got pretty weary of them same mountains, staring me in the face all the time. I didn't have even a dog with me for conversation, so I got to thinking. Thinking is a bad thing, mostly, don't you agree, Ronicky?"

"It sure is," replied Ronicky Doone instantly. "Not a bit of a doubt about it."

"It starts you doubting things," went on Gregg bitterly, "and pretty soon you're even doubting yourself." Here he cast an envious glance at the smooth brow of his companion. "But I guess that never happened to you, Ronicky?"

"You'd be surprised if I told you," said Ronicky.

"Well," went on Bill Gregg, "I got so darned tired of my own thoughts and of myself that I decided something had ought to be done; something to give me new things to think about. So I sat down and went over the whole deal.

"I had to get new ideas. Then I thought of what a gent had told me once. He'd got pretty interested in mining and figured he wanted to know all about how the fancy things was done. So he sent off to some correspondence schools. Well, they're a great bunch. They say: 'Write us a lot of letters and ask us your questions. Before you're through you'll know something you want to know.' See?"

"I see."

"I didn't have anything special I wanted to learn except how to use myself for company when I got tired of solitaire. So I sat down and wrote to this here correspondence school and says: 'I want to do something interesting. How d'you figure that I had better begin?' And what d'you think they answered back?"

"I dunno," said Ronicky, his interest steadily increasing.

"Well, sir, the first thing they wrote back was: 'We have your letter and think that in the first place you had better learn how to write.' That was a queer answer, wasn't it?"

"It sure was." Ronicky swallowed a smile.

"Every time I looked at that letter it sure made me plumb mad. And I looked at it a hundred times a day and come near tearing it up every time. But I didn't," continued Bill.

"Why not?"

"Because it was a woman that wrote it. I told by the hand, after a while!"

"A woman? Go on, Bill. This story sure sounds different from most."

"It ain't even started to get different yet," said Bill gloomily. "Well, that letter made me so plumb mad that I sat down and wrote everything I could think of that a gent would say to a girl to let her know what I thought about her. And what d'you think happened?"

"She wrote you back the prettiest letter you ever seen," suggested Ronicky, "saying as how she'd never meant to make you mad and that if you—"

"Say," broke in Bill Gregg, "did I show that letter to you?"

"Nope; I just was guessing at what a lot of women would do. You see?"

"No, I don't. I could never figure them as close as that. Anyway that's the thing she done, right enough. She writes me a letter that was smooth as oil and suggests that I go on with a composition course to learn how to write."

"Going to have you do books, Bill?"

"I ain't a plumb fool, Ronicky. But I thought it wouldn't do me no harm to unlimber my pen and fire out a few words a day. So I done it. I started writing what they told me to write about, the things that was around me, with a lot of lessons about how you can't use the same word

33

twice on one page, and how terrible bad it is to use too many passive verbs."

"What's a passive verb, Bill?"

"I didn't never figure it out, exactly. However, it seems like they're something that slows you up the way a muddy road slows up a hoss. And then she begun talking about the mountains, and then she begun asking—"

"About you!" suggested Ronicky with a grin.

"Confound you," said Bill Gregg. "How come you guessed that?"

"I dunno. I just sort of scented what was coming."

"Well, anyways, that's what she done. And pretty soon she sent me a snapshot of herself. Well—"

"Lemme see it," said Ronicky Doone calmly.

"I dunno just where it is, maybe," replied Bill Gregg.

"I'll tell you. It's right around your neck, in that nugget locket you wear there."

For a moment Bill Gregg hated the other with his eyes, and then he submitted with a sheepish grin, took off the locket, which was made of one big nugget rudely beaten into shape, and opened it for the benefit of Ronicky Doone. It showed the latter not a beautiful face, but a pretty one with a touch of honesty and pride that made her charming.

"Well, as soon as I got that picture," said Bill Gregg, as he took back the locket, "I sure got excited. Looked to me like that girl was made for me. A lot finer than I could ever be, you see, but simple; no fancy frills, no raving beauty, maybe, but darned easy to look at.

"First thing I done I went in and got a copy of my face made and rushed it right back at her and then—" He stopped dolefully. "What d'you think, Ronicky?"

"I dunno," said Ronicky; "what happened then?"

"Nothing, not a thing. Not a word came back from her to answer that letter I'd sent along."

"Maybe you didn't look rich enough to suit her, Bill."

"I thought that, and I thought it was my ugly face that might of made her change her mind. I thought of pretty near everything else that was bad about me and that she might of read in my face. Sure made me sick for a long time. Somebody else was correcting my lessons, and that made me sicker than ever.

"So I sat down and wrote a letter to the head of the school and told him I'd like to get the address of that first girl. You see, I didn't even know her name. But I didn't get no answer."

Ronicky groaned. "It don't look like the best detective in the world could help you to find a girl when you don't know her name." He added gently: "But maybe she don't want you to find her?"

"I thought that for a long time. Then, a while back, I got a letter from San Francisco, saying that she was coming on a train through these parts and could I be in Stillwater because the train stopped there a couple of minutes. Most like she thought Stillwater was just sort of across the street from me. Matter of fact, I jumped on a hoss, and it took me three days of breaking my neck to get near Stillwater and then—" He stopped and cast a gloomy look on his companion.

"I know," said Ronicky. "Then I come and spoiled the whole party. Sure makes me sick to think about it."

"And now she's plumb gone," muttered Bill Gregg. "I thought maybe the reason I didn't have her correcting my lessons any more was because she'd had to leave the schools and go West. So, right after I got this drilling through the leg, you remember, I wrote a letter?"

"Sure."

"It was to her at the schools, but I didn't get no answer. I guess she didn't go back there after all. She's plumb gone, Ronicky."

The other was silent for a moment. "How much would you give to find her?" he asked suddenly.

"Half my life," said Bill Gregg solemnly.

"Then," said Ronicky, "we'll make a try at it. I got an idea how we can start on the trail. I'm going to go with you, partner. I've messed up considerable, this little game of yours; now I'm going to do what I can to straighten it out. Sometimes two are better than one. Anyway I'm going to stick with you till you've found her or lost her for good. You see?"

Bill Gregg sighed. "You're pretty straight, Ronicky," he said, "but what good does it do for two gents to look for a needle in a haystack? How could we start to hit the trail?"

"This way. We know the train that she took. Maybe we could find the Pullman conductor that was on it, and he might remember her. They got good memories, some of those gents. We'll start to find him, which had ought to be pretty easy."

"Ronicky, I'd never of thought of that in a million years!"

"It ain't thinking that we want now, it's acting. When can you start with me?"

"I'll be fit tomorrow."

"Then tomorrow we start."

Chapter Five

Macklin's Library

Robert Macklin, Pullman conductor, had risen to that eminent position so early in life that the glamour of it had not yet passed away. He was large enough to have passed for a champion wrestler or a burly pugilist, and he was small enough to glory in the smallest details of his work. Having at the age of thirty, through a great deal of luck and a touch of accident, secured his place, he possessed, at least, sufficient dignity to fill it.

He was one of those rare men who carry their dignity with them past the doors of their homes. Robert Macklin's home, during the short intervals when he was off the trains, was in a tiny apartment. It was really one not overly large room, with a little alcove adjoining; but Robert Macklin had seized the opportunity to hang a curtain across the alcove, and, since it was large enough to contain a chair and a bookshelf, he referred to it always as his "library."

He was this morning seated in his library, with his feet protruding through the curtains and resting on the foot of his bed, when the doorbell rang. He surveyed himself in his mirror before he answered it. Having decided that, in his long dressing gown, he was imposing enough, he advanced to the door and slowly opened it.

He saw before him two sun-darkened men whose soft gray hats proclaimed that they were newly come out of the West. The one was a fellow whose face had been made stern by hard work and few pleasures in life. The other was one who, apparently, had never worked at all. There was something about him that impressed Robert Macklin. He might be a young Western millionaire, for instance. Aside from his hat he was dressed with elaborate care. He wore gray spats, and his clothes were obviously well tailored, and his necktie was done in a bow. On the whole he was a very cool, comfortable-looking chap. The handkerchief, which protruded from his breast pocket and showed an edging of red, was a trifle noisy; and the soft gray hat was hardly in keeping, but, on the whole, he was a dashing-looking chap. The bagging trousers and the blunt-toed shoes of his companion were to Robert Macklin a distinct shock. He centered all of his attention instantly on the younger of his two visitors.

"You're Mr. Macklin, I guess," said the handsome man.

"I am," said Macklin, and, stepping back from his door, he invited them in with a sweeping gesture.

There were only two chairs, but the younger of the strangers immediately made himself comfortable on the bed.

"My name's Doone," he said, "and this is Mr. William Gregg. We think that you have some information which we can use. Mind if we fire a few questions?"

"Certainly not," said Robert Macklin. At the same time he began to arm himself with caution. One could never tell.

"Matter of fact," went on Ronicky smoothly, lighting a tailor-made cigarette, while his companion rolled one of his own making, "we are looking for a lady who was on one of your trains. We think you may possibly remember her. Here's the picture."

And, as he passed the snapshot to the Pullman conductor, he went on with the details of the date and the number of the train.

Robert Macklin in the meantime studied the picture carefully. He had a keen eye for faces, but when it came to pretty faces his memory was a veritable lion. He had talked a few moments with this very girl, and she had smiled at him. The memory made Robert Macklin's lips twitch just a trifle, and Ronicky Doone saw it.

Presently the dignitary returned the picture and raised his head from thought. "It is vaguely behind my mind, something about this lady," he said. "But I'm sorry to say, gentlemen, I really don't know you and—"

"Why, don't you know us!" broke in Bill Gregg. "Ain't my partner here just introduced us?"

"Exactly," said Robert Macklin. And his opinion of the two sank a full hundred points. Such grammar proclaimed a ruffian.

"You don't get his drift," Ronicky was explaining to his companion. "I introduced us, but he doesn't know who I am. We should have brought along a letter of introduction." He turned to Macklin. "I am mighty sorry I didn't get one," he said.

It came to Macklin for the fraction of a second that he was being mocked, but he instantly dismissed the foolish thought. Even the rough fellows must be able to recognize a man when they saw one.

"The point is," went on Ronicky gently, "that my friend is very eager for important reasons to see this lady, to find her. And he doesn't even know her name." Here his careful grammar gave out with a crash. "You can't beat a deal like that, eh, Macklin? If you can remember anything about her, her name first, then, where she was bound, who was with her, how tall she is, the color of her eyes, we'd be glad to know anything you know. What can you do for us?"

Macklin cleared his throat thoughtfully. "Gentlemen," he said gravely, "if I knew the purpose for which you are seeking the lady I—"

41

"The purpose ain't to kidnap her, if that's your drift," said Ronicky. "We ain't going to treat her wrong, partner. Out in our part of the land they don't do it. Just shake up your thoughts and see if something about that girl doesn't pop right into your head."

Robert Macklin smiled and carefully shook his head. "It seems to be impossible for me to remember a thing," he asserted.

"Not even the color of her eyes?" asked Ronicky, as he grinned. He went on more gravely: "I'm pretty dead sure that you do remember something about her."

There was just the shade of a threat in the voice of this slender youngster, and Robert Macklin had been an amateur pugilist of much brawn and a good deal of boxing skill. He cast a wary eye on Ronicky; one punch would settle that fellow. The man Gregg might be a harder nut to crack, but it would not take long to finish them both. Robert Macklin thrust his shoulders forward.

"Friends," he said gruffly, "I don't have much time off. This is my day for rest. I have to say good-by."

Ronicky Doone stood up with a yawn. "I thought so," he said to his companion. "Mind the door, Gregg, and see that nobody steps in and busts up my little party."

"What are you going to do?"

"Going to argue with this gent in a way he'll understand a pile better than the chatter we've been making so far." He stepped a long light pace forward. "Macklin, you know what we want to find out. Will you talk?"

A cloud of red gathered before the eyes of Macklin. It was impossible that he must believe his ears, and yet the words still rang there.

"Why, curse your little rat-face!" burst out Robert Macklin, and, stepping in, he leaned forward with a perfect straight left.

Certainly his long vacation from boxing had not ruined his eye or stiffened his muscles. With delight he felt all the big sinews about his shoulders come into play. Straight and true the big fist drove into the face of the smaller man, but Robert Macklin found that he had punched a hole in thin air. It was as if the very wind of the blow had brushed the head of Ronicky Doone to one side, and at the same time he seemed to sway and stagger forward.

A hard lean fist struck Robert Macklin's body. As he gasped and doubled up, clubbing his right fist to land the blow behind the ear of Ronicky Doone, the latter bent back, stepped in and, rising on the toes of both feet, whipped a perfect uppercut that, in ring parlance, rang the bell.

The result was that Robert Macklin, his mouth agape and his eyes dull, stood wabbling slowly from side to side.

"Here!" called Ronicky to his companion at the door. "Grab him on one side, and I'll take the other. He's out on his feet. Get him to that chair." With Gregg's assistance he dragged the bulk of the man there. Macklin was still stunned.

Presently the dull eyes cleared and filled immediately with horror. Big Robert Macklin sank limply back in the chair.

"I've no money," he said. "I swear I haven't a cent in the place. It's in the bank, but if a check will—"

"We don't want your money this trip," said Ronicky. "We want talk, Macklin. A lot of talk and a lot of true talk. Understand? It's about that girl. I saw you grin when you saw the picture; you remember her well enough. Now start talking, and remember this, if you lie, I'll come back here and find out and use this on you."

The eyes of Robert Macklin started from his head, as his gaze concentrated on the black muzzle of the gun. He moistened his white lips and managed to gasp: "Everything I know, of course. I'll tell you everything, word for word. She—she—her name I mean—"

"You're doing fine," said Ronicky. "Keep it up, and you keep away, Bill. When you come at him with that hungry look he thinks you're going to eat him up. Fire away, Macklin."

"What first?"

"What's she look like?"

"Soft brown hair, blue eyes, her mouth—"

"Is a little big. That's all right. You don't have to be polite and lie. We want the truth. How big is she?"

"About five feet and five inches, must weigh around a hundred and thirty pounds."

"You sure are an expert on the ladies, Macklin, and I'll bet you didn't miss her name?"

"Her name?"

"Don't tell me you missed out on that!"

"No. It was—Just a minute!"

"Take your time."

"Caroline."

"Take your time now, Macklin, you're doing fine. Don't get confused. Get the last name right. It's the most important to us."

"I have it, I'm sure. The whole name is Caroline Smith."

There was a groan from Ronicky Doone and another from Bill Gregg.

"That's a fine name to use for trailing a person. Did she say anything more, anything about where she expected to be living in New York?"

"I don't remember any more," said Macklin sullenly, for the spot where Ronicky's fist landed on his jaw was beginning to ache. "I didn't sit down and have any chats with her. She just spoke to me once in a while when I did something for her. I suppose you fellows have some crooked work on hand for her?"

"We're bringing her good news," said Ronicky calmly. "Now see if you can't remember where she said she lived in New York." And he gave added point to his question by pressing the muzzle of the revolver a little closer to the throat of the Pullman conductor. The latter blinked and swallowed hard.

"The only thing I remember her saying was that she could see the East River from her window, I think."

"And that's all you know?"

"Yes, not a thing more about her to save my life."

"Maybe what you know has saved it," said Ronicky darkly.

His victim eyed him with sullen malevolence. "Maybe there'll be a new trick or two in this game before it's finished. I'll never forget you, Doone, and you, Gregg."

"You haven't a thing in the world on us," replied Ronicky.

"I have the fact that you carry concealed weapons."

"Only this time."

"Always! Fellows like you are as lonesome without a gun as they are without a skin."

Ronicky turned at the door and laughed back at the gloomy face, and then they were gone down the steps and into the street.

Chapter Six

The New York Trail

On the train to New York that night they carefully summed up their prospects and what they had gained.

"We started at pretty near nothing," said Ronicky. He was a professional optimist. "We had a picture of a girl, and we knew she was on a certain train bound East, three or four weeks ago. That's all we knew. Now we know her name is Caroline Smith, and that she lives where she can see the East River out of her back window. I guess that narrows it down pretty close, doesn't it, Bill?"

"Close?" asked Bill. "Close, did you say?"

"Well, we know the trail," said Ronicky cheerily. "All we've got to do is to locate the shack that stands beside that trail. For old mountain men like us that ought to be nothing. What sort of a stream is this East River, though?"

Bill Gregg looked at his companion in disgust. He had become so used to regarding Doone as entirely infallible that it amazed and disheartened him to find that there was one topic so large about which Ronicky knew nothing. Perhaps the whole base for the good cheer of Ronicky was his ignorance of everything except the mountain desert.

"A river's a river," went on Ronicky blandly. "And it's got a town beside it, and in the town there's a house that looks over the water. Why, Bill, she's as good as found!"

"New York runs about a dozen miles along the shore of that river," groaned Bill Gregg.

"A dozen miles!" gasped Ronicky. He turned in his seat and stared at his companion. "Bill, you sure are making a man-sized joke. There ain't that much city in the world. A dozen miles of houses, one right next to the other?"

"Yep, and one on top of the other. And that ain't all. Start about the center of that town and swing a twenty-mile line around it, and the end of the line will be passing through houses most of the way."

Ronicky Doone glared at him in positive alarm. "Well," he said, "that's different."

"It sure is. I guess we've come on a wild-goose chase, Ronicky, hunting for a girl named Smith that lives on the bank of the East River!" He laughed bitterly.

"How come you know so much about New York?" asked Ronicky, eager to turn the subject of conversation until he could think of something to cheer his friend.

"Books," said Bill Gregg.

After that there was a long lull in the conversation. That night neither of them slept long, for every rattle and sway of the train was telling them that they were rocking along toward an impossible task. Even the cheer of Ronicky had broken down the next morning, and, though breakfast in the diner restored some of his confidence, he was not the man of the day before.

"Bill," he confided, on the way back to their seats from the diner, "there must be something wrong with me. What is it?"

"I dunno," said Bill. "Why?"

"People been looking at me."

"Ain't they got a right to do that?"

"Sure they have, in a way. But, when they don't seem to see you when you see them, and when they begin looking at you out of the corner of their eyes the minute you turn away, why then it seems to me that they're laughing at you, Bill."

"What they got to laugh about? I'd punch a gent in the face that laughed at me!"

But Ronicky fell into a philosophical brooding. "It can't be done, Bill. You can punch a gent for cussing you, or stepping on your foot, or crowding you, or sneering at you, or talking behind your back, or for a thousand things. But back here in a crowd you can't fight a gent for laughing at you. Laughing is outside the law most anywheres, Bill. It's the one thing you can't answer back except with more ‑ laughing. Even a dog gets sort of sick inside when you laugh at him, and a man is a pile worse. He wants to kill the gent that's laughing, and he wants to kill himself for being laughed at. Well, Bill, that's a good deal stronger than the way they been laughing at me, but they done enough to make me think a bit. They been looking at three things—these here spats, the red rim of my handkerchief sticking out of my pocket, and that soft gray hat, when I got it on."

"Derned if I see anything wrong with your outfit. Didn't they tell you that that was the style back East, to have spats like that on?"

"Sure," said Ronicky, "but maybe they didn't know, or maybe they go with some, but not with me. Maybe I'm kind of too brown and outdoors-looking to fit with spats and handkerchiefs like this."

"Ronicky," said Bill Gregg in admiration, "maybe you ain't read a pile, but you figure things out just like a book."

Their conversation was cut short by the appearance of a drift of houses, and then more and more. From the elevated line on which they ran presently they could look down on block after block of roofs packed close together, or big business structures, as they reached the uptown business sections, and finally Ronicky gasped, as they plunged into utter darkness that roared past the window.

"We go underground to the station," Bill Gregg explained. He was a little startled himself, but his reading had fortified him to a certain extent.

"But is there still some more of New York?" asked Ronicky humbly.

"More? We ain't seen a corner of it!" Bill's superior information made him swell like a frog in the sun. "This is kinder near One Hundredth Street where we dived down. New York keeps right on to First Street, and then it has a lot more streets below that. But that's just the Island of Manhattan. All around there's a lot more. Manhattan is mostly where they work. They live other places."

It was not very long before the train slowed down to make Grand Central Station. On the long platform Ronicky surrendered his suit case to the first porter. Bill Gregg was much alarmed. "What'd you do that for?" he asked, securing a stronger hold on his own valise and brushing aside two or three red caps.

"He asked me for it," explained Ronicky. "I wasn't none too set on giving it to him to carry, but I hated to hurt his feelings. Besides, they're all done up in uniforms. Maybe this is their job."

"But suppose that feller got away out of sight, what would you do? Your brand-new pair of Colts is lying away in it!"

"He won't get out of sight none," Ronicky assured his friend grimly. "I got another Colt with me, and, no matter how fast he runs, a forty-five slug can run a pile faster. But come on, Bill. The word in this town seems to be to keep right on moving."

They passed under an immense, brightly lighted vault and then wriggled through the crowds in pursuit of the astonishingly agile porter. So they came out of the big station to Forty-second Street, where they found themselves confronted by a taxi driver and the question: "Where?"

"I dunno," said Ronicky to Bill. "Your reading tell you anything about the hotels in this here town?"

"Not a thing," said Bill, "because I never figured that I'd be fool enough to come this far away from my home diggings. But here I am, and we don't know nothing."

"Listen, partner," said Ronicky to the driver. "Where's a fair-to-medium place to stop at?"

The taxi driver swallowed a smile that left a twinkle about his eyes which nothing could remove. "What kind of a place? Anywhere from fifty cents to fifty bucks a night."

"Fifty dollars!" exclaimed Bill Gregg. "Can you lay over that, Ronicky? Our wad won't last a week."

"Say, pal," said the taxi driver, becoming suddenly friendly, "I can fix you up. I know a neat little joint where you'll be as snug as you want. They'll stick you about one-fifty per, but you can't beat that price in this town and keep clean."

"Take us there," said Bill Gregg, and they climbed into the machine.

The taxi turned around, shot down Park Avenue, darted aside into the darker streets to the east of the district and came suddenly to a halt.

"Did you foller that trail?" asked Bill Gregg in a chuckling whisper.

"Sure! Twice to the left, then to the right, and then to the left again. I know the number of blocks, too. Ain't no reason for getting rattled just because a joint is strange to us. New York may be tolerable big, but it's got men in it just like we are, and maybe a lot worse kinds."

As they got out of the little car they saw that the taxi driver had preceded them, carrying their suit cases. They followed up a steep pitch of stairs to the first floor of the hotel, where the landing had been widened to form a little office.

"Hello, Bert," said their driver. "I picked up these gentlemen at Grand Central. They ain't wise to the town, so I put 'em next to you. Fix 'em up here?"

"Sure," said Bert, lifting a huge bulk of manhood from behind the desk. He placed his fat hands on the top of it and observed his guests with a smile. "I'll make you right to home here, friends. Thank you, Joe!"

Joe grinned, nodded and, receiving his money from Bill Gregg, departed down the stairs, humming. Their host, in the meantime, had picked up their suit cases and led the way down a hall dimly lighted by two flickering gas jets. Finally he reached a door and led them into a room where the gas had to be lighted. It showed them a cheerless apartment in spite of the red of wall paper and carpet.

"Only three bucks," said the proprietor with the air of one bestowing charity out of the fullness of his heart. "Bathroom only two doors down. I guess you can't beat this layout, gents?"

Bill Gregg glanced once about him and nodded.

"You come up from the South, maybe?" asked the proprietor, lingering at the door.

"West," said Bill Gregg curtly.

"You don't say! Then you boys must be used to your toddy at night, eh?"

"It's a tolerable dry country out there," said Ronicky without enthusiasm.

"All the more reason you need some liquor to moisten it up. Wait till I get you a bottle of rye I got handy." And he disappeared in spite of their protests.

"I ain't a drinking man," said Gregg, "and I know you ain't, but it's sure insulting to turn down a drink in these days!"

Ronicky nodded, and presently the host returned with two glasses, rattling against a tall bottle on a tray.

"Say, when," he said, filling the glasses and keeping on, in spite of their protests, until each glass was full.

"I guess it looks pretty good to you to see the stuff again," he said, stepping back and rubbing his hands like one warmed by the consciousness of a good deed. "It ain't very plentiful around here."

"Well," said Gregg, swinging up his glass, "here's in your eye, Ronicky, and here's to you, sir!"

"Wait," replied Ronicky Doone. "Hold on a minute, Bill. Looks to me like you ain't drinking," he said to the proprietor.

The fat man waved the suggestion aside. "Never touch it," he assured them. "Used to indulge a little in light wines and beers when the country was wet, but when it went dry the stuff didn't mean enough to me to make it worth while dodging the law. I just manage to keep a little of it around for old friends and men out of a dry country."

"But we got a funny habit out in our country. We can't no ways drink unless the gent that's setting them out takes something himself. It ain't done that way in our part of the land," said Ronicky.

"It ain't?"

"Never!"

"Come, come! That's a good joke. But, even if I can't be with you, boys, drink hearty."

Ronicky Doone shook his head. "No joke at all," he said firmly. "Matter of politeness that a lot of gents are terrible hard set on out where we come from."

"Why, Ronicky," protested Bill Gregg, "ain't you making it a little strong? For my part I've drunk twenty times without having the gent that set 'em up touch a thing. I reckon I can do it again. Here's how!"

"Wait!" declared Ronicky Doone. And there was a little jarring ring in his voice that arrested the hand of Bill Gregg in the very act of raising the glass.

Ronicky crossed the room quickly, took a glass from the washstand and, returning to the center table, poured a liberal drink of the whisky into it.

"I dunno about my friend," he went on, almost sternly, to the bewildered hotel keeper. "I dunno about him, but some gents feel so strong about not drinking alone that they'd sooner fight. Well, sir, I'm one of that kind. So I say, there's your liquor. Get rid of it!"

The fat man reached the center table and propped himself against it, gasping. His whole big body seemed to be wilting, as though in a terrific heat. "I dunno!" he murmured. "I dunno what's got into you fellers. I tell you, I never drink."

"You lie, you fat fool!" retorted Ronicky. "Didn't I smell your breath?"

Bill Gregg dropped his own glass on the table and hurriedly came to confront his host by the side of Ronicky.

"Breath?" asked the fat man hurriedly, still gasping more and more heavily for air. "I—I may have taken a small tonic after dinner. In fact, think I did. That's all. Nothing more, I assure you. I—I have to be a sober man in my work."

"You got to make an exception this evening," said Ronicky, more fiercely than ever. "I ought to make you drink all three drinks for being so slow about drinking one!"

"Three drinks!" exclaimed the fat man, trembling violently. "It—it would kill me!"

"I think it would," said Ronicky. "I swear I think it would. And maybe even one will be a sort of a shock, eh?"

He commanded suddenly: "Drink! Drink that glass and clean out the last drop of it, or we'll tie you and pry your mouth open and pour the whole bottle down your throat. You understand?"

A feeble moan came from the throat of the hotel keeper. He cast one frantic glance toward the door and a still more frantic appeal centered on Ronicky Doone, but the face of the latter was as cold as stone.

"Then take your own glasses, boys," he said, striving to smile, as he picked up his own drink.

"You drink first, and you drink alone," declared Ronicky. "Now!"

The movement of his hand was as ominous as if he had whipped out a revolver. The fat man tossed off the glass of whisky and then stood with a pudgy hand pressed against his breast and the upward glance of one who awaits a calamity. Under the astonished eyes of Bill Gregg he turned pale, a sickly greenish pallor. His eyes rolled, and his hand on the table shook, and the arm that supported him sagged.

"Open the window," he said. "The air—there ain't no air. I'm choking—and—"

"Get him some water," cried Bill Gregg, "while I open the window."

"Stay where you are, Bill."

"But he looks like he's dying!"

"Then he's killed himself."

"Gents," began the fat man feebly and made a short step toward them. The step was incompleted. In the middle of it he wavered, put out his arms and slumped upon his side on the floor.

Bill Gregg cried out softly in astonishment and horror, but Ronicky Doone knelt calmly beside the fallen bulk and felt the beating of his heart.

"He ain't dead," he said quietly, "but he'll be tolerably sick for a while. Now come along with me."

"But what's all this mean?" asked Bill Gregg in a whisper, as he picked up his suit case and hurried after Ronicky.

"Doped booze," said Ronicky curtly.

They hurried down the stairs and came out onto the dark street. There Ronicky Doone dropped his suit case and dived into a dark nook beside the entrance. There was a brief struggle. He came out again, pushing a skulking figure before him, with the man's arm twisted behind his back.

"Take off this gent's hat, will you?" asked Ronicky.

Bill Gregg obeyed, too dumb with astonishment to think. "It's the taxi driver!" he exclaimed.

"I thought so!" muttered Ronicky. "The skunk came back here to wait till we were fixed right now. What'll we do with him?"

"I begin to see what's come off," said Bill Gregg, frowning into the white, scowling face of the taxi driver. The man was like a rat, but, in spite of his fear, he did not make a sound.

"Over there!" said Bill Gregg, nodding toward a flight of cellar steps.

They caught the man between them, rushed him to the steps and flung him headlong down. There was a crashing fall, groans and then silence.

"He'll have a broken bone or two, maybe," said Ronicky, peering calmly into the darkness, "but he'll live to trap somebody else, curse him!" And, picking up their suit cases again, they started to retrace their steps.

Chapter Seven

The First Clue

They did not refer to the incidents of that odd reception in New York until they had located a small hotel for themselves, not three blocks away. It was no cheaper, but they found a pleasant room, clean and with electric lights. It was not until they had bathed and were propped up in their beds for a good-night smoke, which cow-punchers love, that Bill Gregg asked: "And what gave you the tip, Ronicky?"

"I dunno. In my business you got to learn to watch faces, Bill. Suppose you sit in at a five-handed game of poker. One gent says everything with his face, while he's picking up his cards. Another gent don't say a thing, but he shows what he's got by the way he moves in his chair, or the way he opens and shuts his hands. When you said something about our wad I seen the taxi driver blink. Right after that he got terrible friendly and said he could steer us to a friend of his that could put us up for the night pretty comfortable. Well, it wasn't hard to put two and two together. Not that I figured anything out. Just was walking on my toes, ready to jump in any direction."

As for Bill Gregg, he brooded for a time on what he had heard, then he shook his head and sighed. "I'd be a mighty helpless kid in this here town if I didn't have you along, Ronicky," he said.

"Nope," insisted Ronicky. "Long as you use another gent for a sort of guide you feel kind of helpless. But, when you step off for yourself, everything is pretty easy. You just were waiting for me to take the lead, or you'd have done just as much by yourself."

Again Bill Gregg sighed, as he shook his head. "If this is what New York is like," he said, "we're in for a pretty bad time. And this is what they call a civilized town? Great guns, they need martial law and a thousand policemen to the block to keep a gent's life and pocketbook safe in this town! First gent we meet tries to bump us off or get our wad. Don't look like we're going to have much luck, Ronicky."

"We saved our hides, I guess."

"That's about all."

"And we learned something."

"Sure."

"Then I figure it was a pretty good night.

"Another thing, Bill. I got an idea from that taxi gent. I figure that whole gang of taxi men are pretty sharp in the eye. What I mean is that we can tramp up and down along this here East River, and now and then we'll talk to some taxi men that do most of their work from stands in them parts of the town. Maybe we can get on her trail that way. Anyways, it's an opening."

"Maybe," said Bill Gregg dubiously. He reached under his pillow. "But I'm sure going to sleep with a gun under my head in this town!" With this remark he settled himself for repose and presently was snoring loudly.

Ronicky presented a brave face to the morning and at once started with Bill Gregg to tour along the East River. That first day Ronicky insisted that they simply walk over the whole ground, so as to become fairly familiar with the scale of their task. They managed to make the trip before night and returned to the hotel, footsore from the hard, hot pavements. There was something unkindly and ungenerous in those pavements, it seemed to Ronicky. He was discovering to his great amazement that the loneliness of the mountain desert is nothing at all compared to the loneliness of the Manhattan crowd.

Two very gloomy and silent cow-punchers ate their dinner that night and went to bed early. But in the morning they began the actual work of their campaign. It was an arduous labor. It meant interviewing in every district one or two storekeepers, and asking the mail carriers for

"Caroline Smith," and showing the picture to taxi drivers. These latter were the men, insisted Ronicky, who would eventually bring them to Caroline Smith. "Because, if they've ever drove a girl as pretty as that, they'll remember for quite a while."

"But half of these gents ain't going to talk to us, even if they know," Bill Gregg protested, after he had been gruffly refused an answer a dozen times in the first morning.

"Some of 'em won't talk," admitted Ronicky, "but that's probably because they don't know. Take 'em by and large, most gents like to tell everything they know, and then some!"

As a matter of fact they met with rather more help than they wanted. In spite of all their efforts to appear casual there was something too romantic in this search for a girl to remain entirely unnoticed. People whom they asked became excited and offered them a thousand suggestions. Everybody, it seemed, had, somewhere, somehow, heard of a Caroline Smith living in his own block, and every one remembered dimly having passed a girl on the street who looked exactly like Caroline Smith. But they went resolutely on, running down a thousand false clues and finding at the end of each something more ludicrous than what had gone before. Maiden ladies with many teeth and big glasses they found; and they discovered, at the ends of the trails on which they were advised to go, young women and old, ugly girls and pretty ones, but never any one who in the slightest degree resembled Caroline Smith.

In the meantime they were working back and forth, in their progress along the East River, from the slums to the better residence districts. They bought newspapers at little stationery stores and worked up chance conversations with the clerks, particularly girl clerks, whenever they could find them.

"Because women have the eye for faces," Ronicky would say, "and, if a girl like Caroline Smith came into the shop, she'd be remembered for a while."

But for ten days they labored without a ghost of a success. Then they noticed the taxi stands along the East Side and worked them as carefully as they could, and it was on the evening of the eleventh day of the search that they reached the first clue.

They had found a taxi drawn up before a saloon, converted into an eating place, and when they went inside they found the driver alone in the restaurant. They worked up the conversation, as they had done a hundred times before. Gregg produced the picture and began showing it to Ronicky.

"Maybe the lady's around here," said Ronicky, "but I'm new in this part of town." He took the picture and turned to the taxi driver. "Maybe you've been around this part of town and know the folks here. Ever see this girl around?" And he passed the picture to the other.

The taxi driver bowed his head over it in a close scrutiny. When he looked up his face was a blank.

"I don't know. Lemme see. I think I seen a girl like her the other day, waiting for the traffic to pass at Seventy-second and Broadway. Yep, she sure was a ringer for this picture." He passed the picture back, and a moment later he finished his meal, paid his check and went sauntering through the door.

"Quick!" said Ronicky, the moment the chauffeur had disappeared. "Pay the check and come along. That fellow knows something."

Bill Gregg, greatly excited, obeyed, and they hurried to the door of the place. They were in time to see the taxicab lurch away from the curb and go humming down the street, while the driver leaned out to the side and looked back.

"He didn't see us," said Ronicky confidently.

"But what did he leave for?"

"He's gone to tell somebody, somewhere, that we're looking for Caroline Smith. Come on!" He stepped out to the curb and stopped a passing taxi. "Follow that machine and keep a block away from it," he ordered.

"Bootlegger?" asked the taxi driver cheerily.

"I don't know, but just drift along behind him till he stops. Can you do that?"

"Watch me!"

And, with Ronicky and Bill Gregg installed in his machine, he started smoothly on the trail.

Straight down the cross street, under the roaring elevated tracks of Second and Third Avenues, they passed, and on First Avenue they turned and darted sharply south for a round dozen blocks, then went due east and came, to a halt after a brief run.

"He's stopped in Beekman Place," said the driver, jerking open the door. "If I run in there he'll see me."

Ronicky stepped from the machine, paid him and dismissed him with a word of praise for his fine trailing. Then he stepped around the corner.

What he saw was a little street closed at both ends and only two or three blocks long. It had the serene, detached air of a village a thousand miles from any great city, with its grave rows of homely houses standing solemnly face to face. Well to the left, the Fifty-ninth Street Bridge swung its great arch across the river, and it led, Ronicky knew, to Long Island City beyond, but here everything was cupped in the village quiet.

The machine which they had been pursuing was drawn up on the right-hand side of the street, looking south, and, even as Ronicky glanced around the corner, he saw the driver leave his seat, dart up a flight of steps and ring the bell.

Ronicky could not see who opened the door, but, after a moment of talk, the chauffeur from the car they had pursued was allowed to enter. And, as he stepped across the threshold, he drew off his cap with a touch of reverence which seemed totally out of keeping with his character as Ronicky had seen it.

"Bill," he said to Gregg, "we've got something. You seen him go up those steps to that house?"

"Sure."

Bill Gregg's eyes were flashing with the excitement. "That house has somebody in it who knows Caroline Smith, and that somebody is excited because we're hunting for her," said Bill. "Maybe it holds Caroline herself. Who can tell that? Let's go see."

"Wait till that taxi driver goes. If he'd wanted us to know about Caroline he'd of told us. He doesn't want us to know and he'd maybe take it pretty much to heart if he knew we'd followed him."

"What he thinks don't worry me none. I can tend to three like him."

"Maybe, but you couldn't handle thirty, and coyotes like him hunt in packs, always. The best fighting pair of coyotes that ever stepped wouldn't have no chance against a lofer wolf, but no lofer wolf could stand off a dozen or so of the little devils. So keep clear of these little rat-faced gents, Bill. They hunt in crowds."

Presently they saw the chauffeur coming down the steps. Even at that distance it could be seen that he was smiling broadly, and that he was intensely pleased with himself and the rest of the world.

Starting up his machine, he swung it around dexterously, as only New York taxi drivers can, and sped down the street by the way he had come, passing Gregg and Ronicky, who had flattened themselves against the fence to keep from being seen. They observed that, while he controlled the car with one hand, with the other he was examining the contents of his wallet.

"Money for him!" exclaimed Ronicky, as soon as the car was out of sight around the corner. "This begins to look pretty thick, Bill. Because he goes and tells them that he's taken us off the trail they not only thank him, but they pay him for it. And, by the face of him, as he went by, they pay him pretty high. Bill, it's easy to figure that they don't want any friend near Caroline Smith, and most like they don't even want us near that house."

"I only want to go near once," said Bill Gregg. "I just want to find out if the girl is there."

"Go break in on 'em?"

"Break in! Ronicky, that's burglary!"

"Sure it is."

"I'll just ask for Caroline Smith at the door."

"Try it."

The irony made Bill Gregg stop in the very act of leaving and glance back. But he went on again resolutely and stamped up the steps to the front door of the house.

It was opened to him almost at once by a woman, for Bill's hat come off. For a moment he was explaining. Then there was a pause in his gestures, as she made the reply. Finally he spoke again, but was cut short by the loud banging of the door.

Bill Gregg drew himself up rigidly and slowly replaced the hat on his head. If a man had turned that trick on him, a .45-caliber slug would have gone crashing through the door in search of him to teach him a Westerner's opinion of such manners.

Ronicky Doone could not help smiling to himself, as he saw Bill Gregg stump stiffly down the stairs, limping a little on his wounded leg, and come back with a grave dignity to the starting point. He was still crimson to the roots of his hair.

"Let's start," he said. "If that happens again I'll be doing a couple of murders in this here little town and getting myself hung."

"What happened?"

"An old hag jerked open the door after I rang the bell. I asked her nice and polite if a lady named Caroline Smith was in the house? 'No,' says she, 'and if she was, what's that to you?' I told her I'd come a long ways to see Caroline. 'Then go a long ways back without seeing Caroline,' says this withered old witch, and she banged the door right in my face. Man, I'm still seeing red. Them words of the old woman were whips, and every one of them sure took off the hide. I used to think that old lady Moore in Martindale was a pretty nasty talker, but this one laid over her a mile. But we're beat, Ronicky. You couldn't get by that old woman with a thousand men."

"Maybe not," said Ronicky Doone, "but we're going to try. Did you look across the street and see a sign a while ago?"

"Which side?"

"Side right opposite Caroline's house."

"Sure. 'Room To Rent.'"

"I thought so. Then that's our room."

"Eh?"

"That's our room, partner, and right at the front window over the street one of us is going to keep watch day and night, till we make sure that Caroline Smith don't live in that house. Is that right?"

"That's a great idea!" He started away from the fence.

"Wait!" Ronicky caught him by the shoulder and held him back. "We'll wait till night and then go and get that room. If Caroline is in the house yonder, and they know we're looking for her, it's easy that she won't be allowed to come out the front of the house so long as we're perched up at the window, waiting to see her. We'll come back tonight and start waiting."

Chapter Eight

Two Apparitions

They found that the room in the house on Beekman Place, opposite that which they felt covered their quarry, could be secured, and they were shown to it by a quiet old gentlewoman, found a big double room that ran across the whole length of the house. From the back it looked down on the lights glimmering on the black East River and across to the flare of Brooklyn; to the left the whole arc of the Fifty-ninth Street Bridge was exposed. In front the windows overlooked Beekman Place and were directly opposite, the front of the house to which the taxi driver had gone that afternoon.

Here they took up the vigil. For four hours one of the two sat with eyes never moving from the street and the windows of the house across the street; and then he left the post, and the other took it.

It was vastly wearying work. Very few vehicles came into the light of the street lamp beneath them, and every person who dismounted from one of them had to be scrutinized with painful diligence.

Once a girl, young and slender and sprightly, stepped out of a taxi, about ten o'clock at night, and ran lightly up the steps of the house. Ronicky caught his friend by the shoulders and dragged him to the window. "There she is now!" he exclaimed.

But the eye of the lover, even though the girl was in a dim light, could not he deceived. The moment he caught her profile, as she turned in opening the door, Bill Gregg shook his head. "That's not the one. She's all different, a pile different, Ronicky."

Ronicky sighed. "I thought we had her," he said. "Go on back to sleep. I'll call you again if anything happens."

But nothing more happened that night, though even in the dull, ghost hours of the early morning they did not relax their vigil. But all the next day there was still no sign of Caroline Smith in the house across the street; no face like hers ever appeared at the windows. Apparently the place was a harmless rooming house of fairly good quality. Not a sign of Caroline Smith appeared even during the second day. By this time the nerves of the two watchers were shattered by the constant strain, and the monotonous view from the front window was beginning to madden them.

"It's proof that she ain't yonder," said Bill Gregg. "Here's two days gone, and not a sign of her yet. It sure means that she ain't in that house, unless she's sick in bed." And he grew pale at the thought.

"Partner," said Ronicky Doone, "if they are trying to keep her away from us they sure have the sense to keep her under cover for as long as two days. Ain't that right? It looks pretty bad for us, but I'm staying here for one solid week, anyway. It's just about our last chance, Bill. We've done our hunting pretty near as well as we could. If we don't land her this trip, I'm about ready to give up."

Bill Gregg sadly agreed that this was their last chance and they must play it to the limit. One week was decided on as a fair test. If, at the end of that time, Caroline Smith did not come out of the house across the street they could conclude that she did not stay there. And then there would be nothing for it but to take the first train back West.

The third day passed and the fourth, dreary, dreary days of unfaltering vigilance on the part of the two watchers. And on the fifth morning even Ronicky Doone sat with his head in his hands at the window, peering through the slit between the drawn curtains which sheltered him from being observed at his spying. When he called out softly, the sound brought Gregg, with one long leap out of the chair where he was sleeping, to the window. There could be no shadow of a doubt about it. There stood Caroline Smith in the door of the house!

She closed the door behind her and, walking to the top of the steps, paused there and looked up and down the street.

Bill Gregg groaned, snatched his hat and plunged through the door, and Ronicky heard the brief thunder of his feet down the first flight of stairs, then the heavy thumps, as he raced around the landing. He was able to trace him down all the three flights of steps to the bottom.

And so swift was that descent that, when the girl, idling down the steps across the street, came onto the sidewalk, Bill Gregg rushed out from the other side and ran toward her.

They made a strange picture as they came to a halt at the same instant, the girl shrinking back in apparent fear of the man, and Bill Gregg stopping by that same show of fear, as though by a blow in the face. There was such a contrast between the two figures that Ronicky Doone might have laughed, had he not been shaking his head with sympathy for Bill Gregg.

For never had the miner seemed so clumsily big and gaunt, never had his clothes seemed so unpressed and shapeless, while his soft gray hat, to which he still clung religiously, appeared hopelessly out of place in contrast with the slim prettiness of the girl. She wore a black straw hat, turned back from her face, with a single big red flower at the side of it; her dress was a tailored gray tweed. The same distinction between their clothes was in their faces, the finely modeled prettiness of her features and the big, careless chiseling of the features of Bill Gregg.

Ronicky Doone did not wonder that, after her first fear, her gesture was one of disdain and surprise.

Bill Gregg had dragged the hat from his head, and the wind lifted his long black hair and made it wild. He went a long, slow step closer to her, with both his hands outstretched.

A strange scene for a street, and Ronicky Doone saw the girl flash a glance over her shoulder and back to the house from which she had just come. Ronicky Doone followed that glance, and he saw, all hidden save the profile of the face, a man standing at an opposite window and smiling scornfully down at that picture in the street.

What a face it was! Never in his life had Ronicky Doone seen a man who, in one instant, filled him with such fear and hatred, such loathing and such dread, such scorn and such terror. The nose was hooked like the nose of a bird of prey; the eyes were long and slanting like those of an Oriental. The face was thin, almost fleshless, so that the bony jaw stood out like the jaw of a death's-head.

As for the girl, the sight of that onlooker seemed to fill her with a new terror. She shrank back from Bill Gregg until her shoulders were almost pressed against the wall of the house. And Ronicky saw her head shake, as she denied Bill the right of advancing farther. Still he pleaded, and still she ordered him away. Finally Bill Gregg drew himself up and bowed to her and turned on his heel.

The girl hesitated a moment. It seemed to Ronicky, in spite of the fact that she had just driven Bill Gregg away, as if she were on the verge of following him to bring him back. For she made a slight outward gesture with one hand.

If this were in her mind, however, it vanished instantly. She turned with a shudder and hurried away down the street.

As for Bill Gregg he bore himself straight as a soldier and came back across the pavement, but it was the erectness of a soldier who has met with a crushing defeat and only preserves an outward resolution, while all the spirit within is crushed.

Ronicky Doone turned gloomily away from the window and listened to the progress of Gregg up the stairs. What a contrast between the ascent and the descent! He had literally flown down. Now his heels clumped out a slow and regular death march, as he came back to the room.

When Gregg opened the door Ronicky Doone blinked and drew in a deep breath at the sight of the poor fellow's face. Gregg had known before that he truly loved this girl whom he had never seen, but he had never dreamed what the strength of that love was. Now, in the very moment of seeing his dream of the girl turned into flesh and blood, he had lost her, and there was something like death in the face of the big miner as he dropped his hat on the floor and sank into a chair.

After that he did not move so much as a finger from the position into which he had fallen limply. His legs were twisted awkwardly, sprawling across the floor in front of him; one long arm dragged down toward the floor, as if there was no strength in it to support the weight of the labor-hardened hands; his chin was fallen against his breast.

When Ronicky Doone crossed to him and laid a kind hand on his shoulder he did not look up. "It's ended," said Bill Gregg faintly. "Now we hit the back trail and forget all about this." He added with a faint attempt at cynicism: "I've just wasted a pile of good money-making time from the mine, that's all."

"H'm!" said Ronicky Doone. "Bill, look me in the eye and tell me, man to man, that you're a liar!" He added: "Can you ever be happy without her, man?"

The cruelty of that speech made Gregg flush and look up sharply. This was exactly what Ronicky Doone wanted.

"I guess they ain't any use talking about that part of it," said Gregg huskily.

"Ain't there? That's where you and me don't agree! Why, Bill, look at the way things have gone! You start out with a photograph of a girl. Now you've followed her, found her name, tracked her clear across the continent and know her street address, and you've given her a chance to see your own face. Ain't that something done?

After you've done all that are you going to give
up now? Not you, Bill! You're going to buck up
and go ahead full steam. Eh?"

Bill Gregg smiled sourly. "D'you know what
she said when I come rushing up and saying:
'I'm Bill Gregg!' D'you know what she said?"

"Well?"

" 'Bill Gregg?' she says. 'I don't remember any
such name!'"

"That took the wind out of me. I only had
enough left to say: 'The gent that was writing
those papers to the correspondence school to
you from the West, the one you sent your picture to and—'

" 'Sent my picture to!' she says and looks as if
the ground had opened under her feet. 'You're
mad!' she says. And then she looks back over
her shoulder as much as to wish she was safe
back in her house!"

"D'you know why she looked back over her
shoulder?"

"Just for the reason I told you."

"No, Bill. There was a gent standing up there
at a window watching her and how she acted.
He's the gent that kept her from writing to you
and signing her name. He's the one who's kept
her in that house. He's the one that knew we
were here watching all the time, that sent out
the girl with exact orders how she should act if
you was to come out and speak to her when you
seen her! Bill, what that girl told you didn't come
out of her own head. It come out of the head of
the gent across the way. When you turned your

back on her she looked like she'd run after you and try to explain. But the fear of that fellow up in the window was too much for her, and she didn't dare. Bill, to get at the girl you got to get that gent I seen grinning from the window."

"Grinning?" asked Bill Gregg, grinding his teeth and starting from his chair. "Was the skunk laughing at me?"

"Sure! Every minute."

Bill Gregg groaned. "I'll smash every bone in his ugly head."

"Shake!" said Ronicky Doone. "That's the sort of talk I wanted to hear, and I'll help, Bill. Unless I'm away wrong, it'll take the best that you and me can do, working together, to put that gent down!"

Chapter Nine

A Bold Venture

But how to reach that man of the smile and the sneer, how, above all, to make sure that he was really the power controlling Caroline Smith, were problems which could not be solved in a moment.

Bill Gregg contributed one helpful idea. "We've waited a week to see her; now that we've seen her let's keep on waiting," he said, and Ronicky agreed.

They resumed the vigil, but it had already been prolonged for such a length of time that it was impossible to keep it as strictly as it had been observed before. Bill Gregg, outworn by the strain of the long watching and the shock of the disappointment of that day, went completely to pieces and in the early evening fell asleep. But Ronicky Doone went out for a light dinner and came back after dark, refreshed and eager for action, only to find that Bill Gregg was incapable of being roused. He slept like a dead man.

Ronicky went to the window and sat alone. Few of the roomers were home in the house opposite. They were out for the evening, or for dinner, at least, and the face of the building was dark and cold, the light from the street lamp glinting unevenly on the windowpanes. He had sat there staring at the old house so many hours in the past that it was beginning to be like a face to him, to be studied as one might study a human being. And the people it sheltered, the old hag who kept the door, the sneering man and Caroline Smith, were to the house like the thoughts behind a man's face, an inscrutable face. But, if one cannot pry behind the mask of the human, at least it is possible to enter a house and find—

At this point in his thoughts Ronicky Doone rose with a quickening pulse. Suppose he, alone, entered that house tonight by stealth, like a burglar, and found what he could find?

He brushed the idea away. Instantly it returned to him. The danger of the thing, and danger there certainly would be in the vicinity of him of the sardonic profile, appealed to him more and more keenly. Moreover, he must go alone. The heavy-footed Gregg would be a poor helpmate on such an errand of stealth.

Ronicky turned away from the window, turned

back to it and looked once more at the tall front of the building opposite; then he started to get ready for the expedition.

The preparations were simple. He put on a pair of low shoes, very light and with rubber heels. In them he could move with the softness and the speed of a cat. Next he dressed in a dark-gray suit, knowing that this is the color hardest to see at night. His old felt hat he had discarded long before in favor of the prevailing style of the average New Yorker. For this night expedition he put on a cap which drew easily over his ears and had a long visor, shadowing the upper part of his face. Since it might be necessary to remain as invisible as possible, he obscured the last bit of white that showed in his costume, with a black neck scarf.

Then he looked in the glass. A lean face looked back at him, the eyes obscured under the cap, a stern, resolute face, with a distinct threat about it. He hardly recognized himself in the face in the glass.

He went to his suit case and brought out his favorite revolver. It was a long and ponderous weapon to be hidden beneath his clothes, but to Ronicky Doone that gun was a friend well tried in many an adventure. His fingers went deftly over it. It literally fell to pieces at his touch, and he examined it cautiously and carefully in all its parts, looking to the cartridges before he assembled the weapon again. For, if it became necessary to shoot this evening, it would be necessary to shoot to kill.

He then strolled down the street, passing the house opposite, with a close scrutiny. A narrow, paved sidewalk ran between it and the house on its right, and all the windows opening on this small court were dark. Moreover, the house which was his quarry was set back several feet from the street, an indentation which would completely hide him from anyone who looked from the street. Ronicky made up his mind at once. He went to the end of the block, crossed over and, turning back on the far side of the street, slipped into the opening between the houses.

Instantly he was in a dense darkness. For five stories above him the two buildings towered, shutting out the starlight. Looking straight up he found only a faint reflection of the glow of the city lights in the sky.

At last he found a cellar window. He tried it and found it locked, but a little maneuvering with his knife enabled him to turn the catch at the top of the lower sash. Then he raised it slowly and leaned into the blackness. Something incredibly soft, tenuous, clinging, pressed at once against his face. He started back with a shudder and brushed away the remnants of a big spider web.

Then he leaned in again. It was an intense blackness. The moment his head was in the opening the sense of listening, which is ever in a house, came to him. There were the strange, musty, underground odors which go with cellars and make men think of death.

However, he must not stay here indefinitely. To be seen leaning in at this window was as bad as to be seen in the house itself. He slipped through the opening at once, and beneath his feet there was a soft crunching of coal. He had come directly into the bin. Turning, he closed the window, for that would be a definite clue to any one who might pass down the alley.

As he stood surrounded by that hostile silence, that evil darkness, he grew somewhat accustomed to the dimness, and he could make out not definite objects, but ghostly outlines. Presently he took out the small electric torch which he carried and examined his surroundings.

The bin had not yet received the supply of winter coal and was almost empty. He stepped out of it into a part of the basement which had been used apparently for storing articles not worth keeping, but too good to be thrown away—an American habit of thrift. Several decrepit chairs and rickety cabinets and old console tables were piled together in a tangled mass. Ronicky looked at them with an unaccountable shudder, as if he read in them the history of the ruin and fall and death of many an old inhabitant of this house. It seemed to his excited imagination that the man with the sneer had been the cause of all the destruction and would be the cause of more.

He passed back through the basement quickly, eager to be out of the musty odors and his gloomy thoughts. He found the storerooms, reached the kitchen stairs and ascended at once. Halfway up the stairs, the door above him suddenly opened and light poured down at him. He saw the flying figure of a cat, a broom behind it, a woman behind the broom.

"Whisht! Out of here, dirty beast!"

The cat thudded against Ronicky's knee, screeched and disappeared below; the woman of the broom shaded her eyes and peered down the steps. "A queer cat!" she muttered, then slammed the door.

It seemed certain to Ronicky that she must have seen him, yet he knew that the blackness of the cellar had probably half blinded her. Besides, he had drawn as far as possible to one side of the steps, and in this way she might easily have overlooked him.

In the meantime it seemed that this way of entering the house was definitely blocked. He paused a moment to consider other plans, but, while he stayed there in thought, he heard the rattle of pans. It decided him to stay a while longer. Apparently she was washing the cooking utensils, and that meant that she was near the close of her work for the evening. In fact, the rim of light, which showed between the door frame and the door, suddenly snapped out, and he heard her footsteps retreating.

Still he delayed a moment or two, for fear she might return to take something which she had forgotten. But the silence deepened above him, and voices were faintly audible toward the front of the house.

That decided Ronicky. He opened the door, blessing the well-oiled hinges which kept it from making any noise, and let a shaft from his pocket lantern flicker across the kitchen floor. The light glimmered on the newly scrubbed surface and showed him a door to his right, opening into the main part of the house.

He passed through it at once and sighed with relief when his foot touched the carpet on the hall beyond. He noted, too, that there was no sign of a creak from the boards beneath his tread. However old that house might be, he was a noble carpenter who laid the flooring, Ronicky thought, as he slipped through the semigloom. For there was a small hall light toward the front, and it gave him an uncertain illumination, even at the rear of the passage.

Now that he was definitely committed to the adventure he wondered more and more what he could possibly gain by it. But still he went on, and, in spite of the danger, it is doubtful if Ronicky would have willingly changed places with any man in the world at that moment.

At least there was not the slightest sense in remaining on the lower floor of the house. He slipped down the shadow of the main stairs, swiftly circled through the danger of the light of the lower hall lamp and started his ascent. Still the carpet muffled every sound which he made in climbing, and the solid construction of the house did not betray him with a single creaking noise.

He reached the first hall. This, beyond doubt, was where he would find the room of the man who sneered—the archenemy, as Ronicky Doone was beginning to think of him. A shiver passed through his lithe, muscular body at the thought of that meeting.

He opened the first door to his left. It was a small closet for brooms and dust cloths and such things. Determining to be methodical he went to the extreme end of the hall and tried that door. It was locked, but, while his hand was still on the knob, turning it in disappointment, a door, higher up in the house, opened and a hum of voices passed out to him. They grew louder, they turned to the staircase from the floor above and commenced to descend at a running pace. Three or four men at least, there must be, by the sound, and perhaps more!

Ronicky started for the head of the stairs to make his retreat, but, just as he reached there, the party turned into the hall and confronted him.

Chapter Ten

Mistaken Identity

To flee down the stairs now would be rank folly. If there happened to be among these fellows a man of the type of him who sneered, a bullet would catch the fugitive long before he reached the bottom of the staircase. And, since he could not retreat, Ronicky went slowly and steadily ahead, for, certainly, if he stood still, he would be spoken to. He would have to rely now on the very dim light in this hall and the shadow of his cap obscuring his face. If these were roomers, perhaps he would be taken for some newcomer.

But he was hailed at once, and a hand was laid on his shoulder.

"Hello, Pete. What's the dope?"

Ronicky shrugged the hand away and went on.

"Won't talk, curse him. That's because the plant went fluey."

"Maybe not; Pete don't talk much, except to the old man."

"Lemme get at him," said a third voice. "Beat it down to Rooney's. I'm going up with Pete and get what he knows."

And, as Ronicky turned onto the next flight of the stairway, he was overtaken by hurrying feet. The other two had already scurried down toward the front door of the house.

"I got some stuff in my room, Pete," said the friendly fellow who had overtaken him. "Come up and have a jolt, and we can have a talk. 'Lefty' and Monahan think you went flop on the job, but I know better, eh? The old man always picks you for these singles; he never gives me a shot at 'em." Then he added: "Here we are!" And, opening a door in the first hall, he stepped to the center of the room and fumbled at a chain that broke loose and tinkled against glass; eventually he snapped on an electric light. Ronicky Doone saw a powerfully built, bull-necked man, with a soft hat pulled far down on his head. Then the man turned.

It was much against the grain for Ronicky Doone to attack a man by surprise, but necessity is a stern ruler. And the necessity which made him strike made him hit with the speed of a snapping whiplash and the weight of a sledge hammer. Before the other was fully turned that iron-hard set of knuckles crashed against the base of his jaw.

He fell without a murmur, without a struggle, Ronicky catching him in his arms to break the weight of the fall. It was a complete knock-out. The dull eyes, which looked up from the floor, saw nothing. The square, rather brutal, face was relaxed as if in sleep, but here was the type of man who would recuperate with great speed.

Ronicky set about the obvious task which lay before him, as fast as he could. In the man's coat pocket he found a handkerchief which, hard knotted, would serve as a gag. The window curtain was drawn with a stout, thick cord. Ronicky slashed off a convenient length of it and secured the hands and feet of his victim, before he turned the fellow on his face.

Next he went through the pockets of the unconscious man who was only now beginning to stir slightly, as life returned after that stunning blow.

It was beginning to come to Ronicky that there was a strange relation between the men of this house. Here were three who apparently started out to work at night, and yet they were certainly not at all the type of night clerks or night-shift engineers or mechanics. He turned over the hand of the man he had struck down. The palm was as soft as his own.

No, certainly not a laborer. But they were all employed by "the old man." Who was he? And was there some relation between all of these and the man who sneered?

At least Ronicky determined to learn all that could be read in the pockets of his victim. There was only one thing. That was a stub-nosed, heavy automatic.

It was enough to make Ronicky Doone sigh with relief. At least he had not struck some peaceful, law-abiding fellow. Any man might carry a gun—Ronicky himself would have been uncomfortable without some sort of weapon about him—but there are guns and guns. This big, ugly automatic seemed specially designed to kill swiftly and surely.

He was considering these deductions when a tap came on the door. Ronicky groaned. Had they come already to find out what kept the senseless victim so long?

"Morgan, oh, Harry Morgan!" called a girl's voice.

Ronicky Doone started. Perhaps—who could tell—this might be Caroline Smith herself, come to tap at the door when he was on the very verge of abandoning the adventure. Suppose it were someone else?

If he ventured out expecting to find Gregg's lady and found instead quite another person— well, women screamed at the slightest provocation, and, if a woman screamed in this house, it seemed exceedingly likely that she would rouse a number of men carrying just such short-nosed, ugly automatics as that which he had just taken from the pocket of Harry Morgan.

In the meantime he must answer something. He could not pretend that the room was empty, for the light must be showing around the door.

"Harry!" called the voice of the girl again. "Do you hear me? Come out! The chief wants you!" And she rattled the door.

Fear that she might open it and, stepping in, see the senseless figure on the floor, alarmed Ronicky. He came close to the door.

"Well?" he demanded, keeping his voice deep, like the voice of Harry Morgan, as well as he could remember it.

"Hurry! The chief, I tell you!"

He snapped out the light and turned resolutely to the door. He felt his faithful Colt, and the feel of the butt was like the touch of a friendly hand before he opened the door.

She was dressed in white and made a glimmering figure in the darkness of the hall, and her hair glimmered, also, almost as if it possessed a light and a life of its own. Ronicky Doone saw that she was a very pretty girl, indeed. Yes, it must be Caroline Smith. The very perfume of young girlhood breathed from her, and very sharply and suddenly he wondered why he should be here to fight the battle of Bill Gregg in this matter—Bill Gregg who slept peacefully and stupidly in the room across the street!

She had turned away, giving him only a side glance, as he came out. "I don't know what's on, something big. The chief's going to give you your big chance—with me."

Ronicky Doone grunted.

"Don't do that," exclaimed the girl impatiently. "I know you think Pete is the top of the world, but that doesn't mean that you can make a good imitation of him. Don't do it, Harry. You'll pass by yourself. You don't need a make-up, and not Pete's on a bet."

They reached the head of the stairs, and Ronicky Doone paused. To go down was to face the mysterious chief whom he had no doubt was the old man to whom Harry Morgan had already referred. In the meantime the conviction grew that this was indeed Caroline Smith. Her free-and-easy way of talk was exactly that of a girl who might become interested in a man whom she had never seen, merely by letters.

"I want to talk to you," said Ronicky, muffling his voice. "I want to talk to you alone."

"To me?" asked the girl, turning toward him. The light from the hall lamp below gave Ronicky the faintest hint of her profile.

"Yes."

"But the chief?"

"He can wait."

She hesitated, apparently drawn by curiosity in one direction, but stopped by another thought. "I suppose he can wait, but, if he gets stirred up about it—oh, we'll, I'll talk to you—but nothing foolish, Harry. Promise me that?"

"Yes."

"Slip into my room for a minute." She led the way a few steps down the hall, and he followed her through the door, working his mind frantically in an effort to find words with which to open his speech before she should see that he was not Harry Morgan and cry out to alarm the

house. What should he say? Something about
Bill Gregg at once, of course. That was the thing.

The electric light snapped on at the far side of
the room. He saw a dressing table, an Empire
bed covered with green-figured silk, a pleasant
rug on the floor, and, just as he had gathered an
impression of delightful femininity from these
furnishings, the girl turned from the lamp on
the dressing table, and he saw—not Caroline
Smith, but a bronze-haired beauty, as different
from Bill Gregg's lady as day is from night.

Chapter Eleven

A Cross-Examination

He was conscious then only of green-blue eyes, very wide, very bright, and lips that parted on a word and froze there in silence. The heart of Ronicky Doone leaped with joy; he had passed the crisis in safety. She had not cried out.

"You're not—" he had said in the first moment.

"I am not who?" asked the girl with amazing steadiness. But he saw her hand go back to the dressing table and open, with incredible deftness and speed, the little top drawer behind her.

"Don't do that!" said Ronicky softly, but sharply. "Keep your hand off that table, lady, if you don't mind."

She hesitated a fraction of a second. In that

moment she seemed to see that he was in earnest, and that it would be foolish to tamper with him.

"Stand away from that table; sit down yonder."

Again she obeyed without a word. Her eyes, to be sure, flickered here and there about the room, as though they sought some means of sending a warning to her friends, or finding some escape for herself. Then her glance returned to Ronicky Doone.

"Well," she said, as she settled in the chair. "Well?"

A world of meaning in those two small words—a world of dread controlled. He merely stared at her thoughtfully.

"I hit the wrong trail, lady," he said quietly. "I was looking for somebody else."

She started. "You were after—" She stopped.

"That's right, I guess," he admitted.

"How many of you are there?" she asked curiously, so curiously that she seemed to be forgetting the danger. "Poor Carry Smith with a mob—" She stopped suddenly again. "What did you do to Harry Morgan?"

"I left him safe and quiet," said Ronicky Doone.

The girl's face hardened strangely. "What you are, and what your game is I don't know," she said. "But I'll tell you this: I'm letting you play as if you had all the cards in the deck. But you haven't. I've got one ace that'll take all your trumps. Suppose I call—once—what'll happen to you, pal?"

"You don't dare call," he said.

"Don't dare me," said the girl angrily. "I hate a dare worse than anything in the world, almost." For a moment her green-blue eyes were pools of light flashing angrily at him.

Into the hand of Ronicky Doone, with that magic speed and grace for which his fame was growing so great in the mountain desert, came the long, glimmering body of the revolver, and, holding it at the hip, he threatened her.

She shrank back at that, gasping. For there was an utter surety about this man's handling of the weapon. The heavy gun balanced and steadied in his slim fingers, as if it were no more than a feather's weight.

"I'm talking straight, lady," said Ronicky Doone. "Sit down—pronto!"

In the very act of obedience she straightened again. "It's bluff," she said. "I'm going through that door!" Straight for the door she went, and Ronicky Doone set his teeth.

"Go back!" he commanded. He glided to the door and blocked her way, but the gun hung futile in his hand.

"It's easy to pull a gun, eh?" said the girl, with something of a sneer. "But it takes nerve to use it. Let me through this door!"

"Not in a thousand years," said Ronicky.

She laid her hand on the door and drew it back—it struck his shoulder—and Ronicky gave way with a groan and stood with his head bowed. Inwardly he cursed himself. Doubtless she was used to men who bullied her, as if she were another man of an inferior sort. Doubtless she despised him for his weakness. But, though he gritted his teeth, he could not make himself firm. Those old lessons which sink into a man's soul in the West came back to him and held him. In the helpless rage which possessed him he wanted battle above all things in the world. If half a dozen men had poured through the doorway he would have rejoiced. But this one girl was enough to make him helpless.

He looked up in amazement. She had not gone; in fact, she had closed the door slowly and stood with her back against it, staring at him in a speechless bewilderment.

"What sort of a man are you?" asked the girl at last.

"A fool," said Ronicky slowly. "Go out and round up your friends; I can't stop you."

"No," said the girl thoughtfully, "but that was a poor bluff at stopping me."

He nodded. And she hesitated still, watching his face closely.

"Listen to me," she said suddenly. "I have two minutes to talk to you, and I'll give you those two minutes. You can use them in getting out of the house—I'll show you a way—or you can use them to tell me just why you've come."

In spite of himself Ronicky smiled. "Lady," he said, "if a rat was in a trap d'you think he'd stop very long between a chance of getting clear and a chance to tell how he come to get into the place?"

"I have a perfectly good reason for asking," she answered. "Even if you now get out of the house safely you'll try to come back later on."

"Lady," said Ronicky, "do I look as plumb foolish as that?"

"You're from the West," she said in answer to his slang.

"Yes."

She considered the straight-looking honesty of his eyes. "Out West," she said, "I know you men are different. Not one of the men I know here would take another chance as risky as this, once they were out of it. But out there in the mountains you follow long trails, trails that haven't anything but a hope to lead you along them? Isn't that so?"

"Maybe," admitted Ronicky. "It's the fever out of the gold days, lady. You start out chipping rocks to find the right color; maybe you never find the right color; maybe you never find a streak of pay stuff, but you keep on trying. You're always just sort of around the corner from making a big strike."

She nodded, smiling again, and the smiles changed her pleasantly, it seemed to Ronicky Doone. At first she had impressed him almost as a man, with her cold, steady eyes, but now she was all woman, indeed.

"That's why I say that you'll come back. You won't give up with one failure. Am I right?"

He shrugged his shoulders. "I dunno. If the trail fever hits me again—maybe I would come back."

"You started to tell me. It's because of Caroline Smith?"

"Yes."

"You don't have to talk to me," said the girl. "As a matter of fact I shouldn't be here listening to you. But, I don't know why, I want to help you. You—you are in love with Caroline?"

"No," said Ronicky.

Her expression grew grave and cold again. "Then why are you here hunting for her? What do you want with her?"

"Lady," said Ronicky, "I'm going to show you the whole layout of the cards. Maybe you'll take what I say right to headquarters—the man that smiles—and block my game."

"You know him?" she asked sharply.

Apparently that phrase, "the man who smiles," was enough to identify him.

"I've seen him. I dunno what he is, I dunno what you are, lady, but I figure that you and Caroline Smith and everybody else in this house is under the thumb of the gent that smiles."

Her eyes darkened with a shadow of alarm. "Go on," she said curtly.

"I'm not going on to guess about what you all are. All I know is what I'm here trying to do. I'm not working for myself. I'm working for a partner."

She started. "That's the second man, the one who stopped her on the street today?"

"You're pretty well posted," replied Ronicky. "Yes, that's the one. He started after Caroline Smith, not even knowing her name—with just a picture of her. We found out that she lived in sight of the East River, and pretty soon we located her here."

"And what are you hoping to do?"

"To find her and talk to her straight from the shoulder and tell her what a pile Bill has done to get to her—and a lot of other things."

"Can't he find her and tell her those things for himself?"

"He can't talk," said Ronicky. "Not that I'm a pile better, but I could talk better for a friend than he could talk for himself, I figure. If things don't go right then I'll know that the trouble is with the gent with the smile."

"And then?" asked the girl, very excited and grave.

"I'll find him," said Ronicky Doone.

"And—"

"Lady," he replied obliquely, "because I couldn't use a gun on a girl ain't no sign that I can't use it on a gent!"

"I've one thing to tell you," she said, breaking in swiftly on him. "Do what you want—take all the chances you care to—but, if you value your life and the life of your friend, keep away from the man who smiles."

"I'll have a fighting chance, I guess," said Ronicky quietly.

"You'll have no chance at all. The moment he knows your hand is against him, I don't care how brave or how clever you are, you're doomed!"

She spoke with such a passion of conviction that she flushed, and a moment later she was shivering. It might have been the draft from the window which made her gather the hazy-green mantle closer about her and glance over her shoulder; but a grim feeling came to Ronicky Doone that the reason why the girl trembled and her eyes grew wide, was that the mention of "the man who smiles" had brought the thought of him into the room like a breath of cold wind.

"Don't you see," she went on gently, "that I like you? It's the first and the last time that I'm going to see you, so I can talk. I know you're honest, and I know you're brave. Why, I can see your whole character in the way you've stayed by your friend; and, if there's a possible way of helping you, I'll do it. But you must promise me first that you'll never cross the man with the sneer, as you call him."

"There's a sort of a fate in it," said Ronicky slowly. "I don't think I could promise. There's a chill in my bones that tells me I'm going to meet up with him one of these days."

She gasped at that, and, stepping back from him, she appeared to be searching her mind to discover—something which would finally and completely convince him. At length she found it.

"Do I look to you like a coward?" she said. "Do I seem to be weak-kneed?"

He shook his head.

"And what will a woman fight hardest for?"

"For the youngsters she's got," said Ronicky after a moment's thought. "And, outside of that, I suppose a girl will fight the hardest to marry the gent she loves."

"And to keep from marrying a man she doesn't love, as she'd try to keep from death?"

"Sure," said Ronicky. "But these days a girl don't have to marry that way."

"I am going to marry the man with the sneer," she said simply enough, and with dull, patient eyes she watched the face of Ronicky wrinkle and grow pale, as if a heavy fist had struck him.

"You?" he asked. "You marry him?"

"Yes," she whispered.

"And you hate the thought of him!"

"I—I don't know. He's kind—"

"You hate him," insisted Ronicky. "And he's to have you, that cold-eyed snake, that devil of a man?" He moved a little, and she turned toward him, smiling faintly and allowing the light to come more clearly and fully on her face. "You're meant for a king o' men, lady; you got the queen in you—it's in the lift of your head. When you find the gent you can love, why, lady, he'll be pretty near the richest man in the world!"

The ghost of a flush bloomed in her cheeks, but her faint smile did not alter, and she seemed to be hearing him from far away. "The man with the sneer," she said at length, "will never talk to me like that, and still—I shall marry him."

"Tell me your name," said Ronicky Doone bluntly.

"My name is Ruth Tolliver."

"Listen to me, Ruth Tolliver: If you was to live a thousand years, and the gent with the smile was to keep going for two thousand, it'd never come about that he could ever marry you."

She shook her head, still watching him as from a distance.

"If I've crossed the country and followed a hard trail and come here tonight and stuck my head in a trap, as you might say, for the sake of a gent like Bill Gregg—fine fellow though he is—what d'you think I would do to keep a girl like you from life-long misery?"

And he dwelt on the last word until the girl shivered.

"It's what it means," said Ronicky Doone, "life-long misery for you. And it won't happen—it can't happen."

"Are you mad—are you quite mad?" asked the girl. "What on earth have I and my affairs got to do with you? Who are you?"

"I dunno," said Ronicky Doone. "I suppose you might say I'm a champion of lost causes, lady. Why have I got something to do with you? I'll tell you why: Because, when a girl gets past being just pretty and starts in being plumb beautiful, she lays off being the business of any one gent— her father or her brother—she starts being the business of the whole world. You see? They come like that about one in ten million, and I figure you're that one, lady."

The far away smile went out. She was looking at him now with a sort of sad wonder. "Do you know what I am?" she said gravely.

"I dunno," said Ronicky, "and I don't care. What you do don't count. It's the inside that matters, and the inside of you is all right. Lady, so long as I can sling a gun, and so long as my name is Ronicky Doone, you ain't going to marry the gent with the smile."

If he expected an outbreak of protest from her he was mistaken. For what she said was: "Ronicky Doone! Is that the name? Ronicky Doone!" Then she smiled up at him. "I'm within one ace of being foolish and saying—But I won't."

She made a gesture of brushing a mist away from her and then stepped back a little. "I'm going down to see the man with the smile, and I'm going to tell him that Harry Morgan is not in his room, that he didn't answer my knock, and then that I looked around through the house and didn't find him. After that I'm coming back here, Ronicky Doone, and I'm going to try to get an opportunity for you to talk to Caroline Smith."

"I knew you'd change your mind," said Ronicky Doone.

"I'll even tell you why," she said. "It isn't for your friend who's asleep, but it's to give you a chance to finish this business and come to the end of this trail and go back to your own country. Because, if you stay around here long, there'll be trouble, a lot of trouble, Ronicky Doone. Now stay here and wait for me. If anyone taps at the door, you'd better slip into that closet in the corner. Will you wait?"

"Yes."

"And you'll trust me?"

"To the end of the trail, lady."

She smiled at him again and was gone.

Now the house was perfectly hushed. He went to the window and looked down to the quiet street with all its atmosphere of some old New England village and eternal peace. It seemed impossible that in the house behind him there were—

He caught his breath. Somewhere in the house the muffled sound of a struggle rose. He ran to the door, thinking of Ruth Tolliver at once, and then he shrank back again, for a door was slammed open, and a voice shouted—the voice of a man: "Help! Harrison! Lefty! Jerry!"

Other voices answered far away; footfalls began to sound. Ronicky Doone knew that Harry Morgan, his victim, had at last recovered and managed to work the cords off his feet or hands, or both.

Ronicky stepped back close to the door of the closet and waited. It would mean a search, probably, this discovery that Morgan had been struck down in his own room by an unknown intruder. And a search certainly would be started at once. First there was confusion, and then a clear, musical man's voice began to give orders: "Harrison, take the cellar. Lefty, go up to the roof. The rest of you take the rooms one by one."

The search was on.

"Don't ask questions," was the last instruction. "When you see someone you don't know, shoot on sight, and shoot to kill. I'll do the explaining to the police—you know that. Now scatter, and the man who brings him down I'll remember. Quick!"

There was a new scurry of footfalls. Ronicky Doone heard them approach the door of the girl's room, and he slipped into the closet. At once a cloud of soft, cool silks brushed about him, and he worked back until his shoulders had touched the wall at the back of the closet. Luckily the enclosure was deep, and the clothes were hanging thickly from the racks. It was sufficient to conceal him from any careless searcher, but it would do no good if any one probed; and certainly these men were not the ones to search carelessly.

In the meantime it was a position which made Ronicky grind his teeth. To be found skulking among woman's clothes in a closet—to be dragged out and stuck in the back, no doubt, like a rat, and thrown into the river, that was an end for Ronicky Doone indeed!

He was on the verge of slipping out and making a mad break for the door of the house and trying to escape by taking the men by surprise, when he heard the door of the girl's room open.

"Some ex-pugilist," he heard a man's voice saying, and he recognized it at once as belonging to him who had given the orders. He recognized, also, that it must be the man with the sneer.

"You think he was an amateur robber and an expert prize fighter?" asked Ruth Tolliver.

It seemed to Ronicky Doone that her voice was perfectly controlled and calm. Perhaps it was her face that betrayed emotion, for after a moment of silence, the man answered.

"What's the matter? You're as nervous as a child tonight, Ruth?"

"Isn't there reason enough to make me nervous?" she demanded. "A robber—Heaven knows what—running at large in the house?"

"H'm!" murmured the man. "Devilish queer that you should get so excited all at once. No, it's something else. I've trained you too well for you to go to pieces like this over nothing. What is it, Ruth?"

There was no answer. Then the voice began again, silken-smooth and gentle, so gentle and kindly that Ronicky Doone started. "In the old days you used to keep nothing from me; we were companions, Ruth. That was when you were a child. Now that you are a woman, when you feel more, think more, see more, when our companionship should be like a running stream, continually bringing new things into my life, I find barriers between us. Why is it, my dear?"

Still there was no answer. The pulse of Ronicky Doone began to quicken, as though the question had been asked him, as though he himself were fumbling for the answer.

"Let us talk more freely," went on the man. "Try to open your mind to me. There are things which you dislike in me; I know it. Just what those things are I cannot tell, but we must break down these foolish little barriers which are appearing more and more every day. Not that I mean to intrude myself on you every moment of your life. You understand that, of course?"

"Of course," said the girl faintly.

"And I understand perfectly that you have passed out of childhood into young womanhood, and that is a dreamy time for a girl. Her body is formed at last, but her mind is only half formed. There is a pleasant mist over it. Very well, I don't wish to brush the mist away. If I did that I would take half that charm away from you—that elusive incompleteness which Fragonard and Watteau tried to imitate, Heaven knows with how little success. No, I shall always let you live your own life. All that I ask for, my dear, are certain meeting places. Let us establish them before it is too late, or you will find one day that you have married an old man, and we shall have silent dinners. There is nothing more wretched than that. If it should come about, then you will begin to look on me as a jailer. And—"

"Don't!"

"Ah," said he very tenderly, "I knew that I was feeling toward the truth. You are shrinking from me, Ruth, because you feel that I am too old."

"No, no!"

Here a hand pounded heavily on the door.

"The idiots have found something," said the man of the sneer. "And now they have come to talk about their cleverness, like a rooster crowing over a grain of corn." He raised his voice. "Come in!"

And Ronicky Doone heard a panting voice a moment later exclaim: "We've got him!"

Chapter Twelve

The Strange Bargain

Ronicky drew his gun and waited. "Good," said the man of the sneer. "Go ahead."

"It was down in the cellar that we found the first tracks. He came in through the side window and closed it after him."

"That dropped him into the coal bin. Did he get coal dust on his shoes?"

"Right; and he didn't have sense enough to wipe it off."

"An amateur—a rank amateur! I told you!" said the man of the sneer, with satisfaction. "You followed his trail?"

"Up the stairs to the kitchen and down the hall and up to Harry's room."

"We already knew he'd gone there."

"But he left that room again and came down the hall."

"Yes. The coal dust was pretty well wiped off by that time, but we held a light close to the carpet and got the signs of it."

"And where did it lead?"

"Right to this room!"

Ronicky stepped from among the smooth silks and pressed close to the door of the closet, his hand on the knob. The time had almost come for one desperate attempt to escape, and he was ready to shoot to kill.

A moment of pause had come, a pause which, in the imagination of Ronicky, was filled with the approach of both the men toward the door of the closet.

Then the man of the sneer said: "That's a likely story!"

"I can show you the tracks."

"H'm! You fool, they simply grew dim when they got to this door. I've been here for some time. Go back and tell them to hunt some more. Go up to the attic and search there. That's the place an amateur would most likely hide."

The man growled some retort and left, closing the door heavily behind him, while Ronicky Doone breathed freely again for the first time.

"Now," said the man of the sneer, "tell me the whole of it, Ruth."

Ronicky set his teeth. Had the clever devil guessed at the truth so easily? Had he sent his follower away, merely to avoid having it known

111

that a man had taken shelter in the room of the girl he loved?

"Go on," the leader was repeating. "Let me hear the whole truth."

"I—I—" stammered the girl, and she could say no more.

The man of the sneer laughed unpleasantly. "Let me help you. It was somebody you met somewhere—on the train, perhaps, and you couldn't help smiling at him, eh? You smiled so much, in fact, that he followed you and found that you had come here. The only way he could get in was by stealth. Is that right? So he came in exactly that way, like a robber, but really only to keep a tryst with his lady love? A pretty story, a true romance! I begin to see why you find me such a dull fellow, my dear girl."

"John—" began Ruth Tolliver, her voice shaking.

"Tush," he broke in as smoothly as ever. "Let me tell the story for you and spare your blushes. When I sent you for Harry Morgan you found Lochinvar in the very act of slugging the poor fellow. You helped him tie Morgan; then you took him here to your room; although you were glad to see him, you warned him that it was dangerous to play with fire—fire being me. Do I gather the drift of the story fairly well? Finally you have him worked up to the right pitch. He is convinced that a retreat would be advantageous, if possible. You show him that it is possible. You point out the ledge under your window and the easy way of working to the ground. Eh?"

"Yes," said the girl unevenly. "That is—"

"Ah!" murmured the man of the sneer. "You seem rather relieved that I have guessed he left the house. In that case—"

Ronicky Doone had held the latch of the door turned back for some time. Now he pushed it open and stepped out. He was only barely in time, for the man of the sneer was turning quickly in his direction, since there was only one hiding place in the room.

He was brought up with a shock by the sight of Ronicky's big Colt, held at the hip and covering him with absolute certainty. Ruth Tolliver did not cry out, but every muscle in her face and body seemed to contract, as if she were preparing herself for the explosion.

"You don't have to put up your hands," said Ronicky Doone, wondering at the familiarity of the face of the man of the sneer. He had brooded on it so often in the past few days that it was like the face of an old acquaintance. He knew every line in that sharp profile.

"Thank you," responded the leader, and, turning to the girl, he said coldly: "I congratulate you on your good taste. A regular Apollo, my dear Ruth."

He turned back to Ronicky Doone. "And I suppose you have overhead our entire conversation?"

"The whole lot of it," said Ronicky, "though I wasn't playing my hand at eavesdropping. I couldn't help hearing you, partner."

The man of the sneer looked him over leisurely. "Western," he said at last, "decidedly Western.

Are you staying long in the East, my friend?"

"I dunno," said Ronicky Doone, smiling faintly at the coolness of the other. "What do you think about it?"

"Meaning that I'm liable to put an end to your stay?"

"Maybe!"

"Tush, tush! I suppose Ruth has filled your head with a lot of rot about what a terrible fellow I am. But I don't use poison, and I don't kill with mysterious X-rays. I am, as you see, a very quiet and ordinary sort."

Ronicky Doone smiled again. "You just oblige me, partner," he replied in his own soft voice. "Just stay away from the walls of the room—don't even sit down. Stand right where you are."

"You'd murder me if I took another step?" asked the man of the sneer, and a contemptuous and sardonic expression flitted across his face for the first time.

"I'd sure blow you full of lead," said Ronicky fervently. "I'd kill you like a snake, stranger, which I mostly think you are. So step light, and step quick when I talk."

"Certainly," said the other, bowing. "I am entirely at your service." He turned a little to Ruth. "I see that you have a most determined cavalier. I suppose he'll instantly abduct you and sweep you away from beneath my eyes?"

She made a vague gesture of denial.

"Go ahead," said the leader. "By the way, my name is John Mark."

"I'm Doone—some call me Ronicky Doone."

"I'm glad to know you, Ronicky Doone. I imagine that name fits you. Now tell me the story of why you came to this house; of course it wasn't to see a girl!"

"You're wrong! It was."

"Ah?" In spite of himself the face of John Mark wrinkled with pain and suspicious rage.

"I came to see a girl, and her name, I figure, is Caroline Smith."

Relief, wonder, and even a gleam of outright happiness shot into the eyes of John Mark. "Caroline? You came for that?" Suddenly he laughed heartily, but there was a tremor of emotion in that laughter. The perfect torture, which had been wringing the soul of the man of the sneer, projected through the laughter.

"I ask your pardon, my dear," said John Mark to Ruth. "I should have guessed. You found him; he confessed why he was here; you took pity on him—and—" He brushed a hand across his forehead and was instantly himself, calm and cool.

"Very well, then. It seems I've made an ass of myself, but I'll try to make up for it. Now what about Caroline? There seems to be a whole host of you Westerners annoying her."

"Only one: I'm acting as his agent."

"And what do you expect?"

"I expect that you will send for her and tell her that she is free to go down with me—leave this house—and take a ride or a walk with me."

"As much as that? If you have to talk to her, why not do the talking here?"

"I dunno," replied Ronicky Doone. "I figure

she'd think too much about you all the time."

"The basilisk, eh?" asked John Mark. "Well, you are going to persuade her to go to Bill Gregg?"

"You know the name, eh?"

"Yes, I have a curious stock of useless information."

"Well, you're right; I'm going to try to get her back for Bill."

"But you can't expect me to assent to that?"

"I sure do."

"And why? This Caroline Smith may be a person of great value to me."

"I have no doubt she is, but I got a good argument."

"What is it?"

"The gun, partner."

"And, if you couldn't get the girl—but see how absurd the whole thing is, Ronicky Doone! I send for the girl; I request her to go down with you to the street and take a walk, because you wish to talk to her. Heavens, man, I can't persuade her to go with a stranger at night! Surely you see that!"

"I'll do that persuading," said Ronicky Doone calmly.

"And, when you're on the streets with the girl, do you suppose I'll rest idle and let you walk away with her?"

"Once we're outside of the house, Mark," said Ronicky Doone, "I don't ask no favors. Let your men come on. All I got to say is that I come from a county where every man wears a gun and has to learn how to use it. I ain't terrible backward with the trigger finger, John Mark. Not that I figure on bragging, but I want you to pick good men for my trail and tell 'em to step soft. Is that square?"

"Aside from certain idiosyncracies, such as your manner of paying a call by way of a cellar window, I think you are the soul of honor, Ronicky Doone. Now may I sit down?"

"Suppose we shake hands to bind the bargain," said Ronicky. "You send for Caroline Smith; I'm to do the persuading to get her out of the house. We're safe to the doors of the house; the minute we step into the street, you're free to do anything you want to get either of us. Will you shake on that?"

For a moment the leader hesitated, then his fingers closed over the extended hand of Ronicky Doone and clamped down on them like so many steel wires contracting. At the same time a flush of excitement and fierceness passed over the face of John Mark. Ronicky Doone, taken utterly by surprise, was at a great disadvantage. Then he put the whole power of his own hand into the grip, and it was like iron meeting iron. A great rage came in the eyes of John Mark; a great wonder came in the eyes of the Westerner. Where did John Mark get his sudden strength?

"Well," said Ronicky, "we've shaken hands, and now you can do what you please! Sit down, leave the room—anything." He shoved his gun away in his clothes. That brought a start from John Mark and a flash of eagerness, but he repressed the idea, after a single glance at the girl.

"We've shaken hands," he admitted slowly, as though just realizing the full extent of the meaning of that act. "Very well, Ronicky, I'll send for Caroline Smith, and more power to your tongue, but you'll never get her away from this house without force."

Chapter Thirteen

Doone Wins

A servant answered the bell almost at once. "Tell Miss Smith that she's wanted in Miss Tolliver's room," said Mark, and, when the servant disappeared, he began pacing up and down the room. Now and then he cast a sharp glance to the side and scrutinized the face of Ronicky Doone. With Ruth's permission, the latter had lighted a cigarette and was smoking it in bland enjoyment. Again the leader paused directly before the girl, and, with his feet spread and his head bowed in an absurd Napoleonic posture, he considered every feature of her face. The uncertain smile, which came trembling on her face, elicited no response from Mark.

She dreaded him, Ronicky saw, as a slave

dreads a cruel master. Still she had a certain affection for him, partly as the result of many benefactions, no doubt, and partly from long acquaintance; and, above all, she respected his powers of mind intensely. The play of emotion in her face—fear, anger, suspicion—as John Mark paced up and down before her, was a study.

With a secret satisfaction Ronicky Doone saw that her glances continually sought him, timidly, curiously. All vanity aside, he had dropped a bomb under the feet of John Mark, and some day the bomb might explode.

There was a tap at the door, it opened and Caroline Smith entered in a dressing gown. She smiled brightly at Ruth and wanly at John Mark, then started at the sight of the stranger.

"This," said John Mark, "is Ronicky Doone."

The Westerner rose and bowed.

"He has come," said John Mark, "to try to persuade you to go out for a stroll with him, so that he can talk to you about that curious fellow, Bill Gregg. He is going to try to soften your heart, I believe, by telling you all the inconveniences which Bill Gregg has endured to find you here. But he will do his talking for himself. Just why he has to take you out of the house, at night, before he can talk to you is, I admit, a mystery to me. But let him do the persuading."

Ronicky Doone turned to his host, a cold gleam in his eyes. His case had been presented in such a way as to make his task of persuasion almost impossible. Then he turned back and looked at the girl. Her face was a little pale, he thought, but perfectly composed.

"I don't know Bill Gregg," she said simply. "Of course, I'm glad to talk to you, Mr. Doone, but why not here?"

John Mark covered a smile of satisfaction, and the girl looked at him, apparently to see if she had spoken correctly. It was obvious that the leader was pleased, and she glanced back at Ronicky, with a flush of pleasure.

"I'll tell you why I can't talk to you in here," said Ronicky gently. "Because, while you're under the same roof with this gent with the sneer"—he turned and indicated Mark, sneering himself as he did so—"you're not yourself. You don't have a halfway chance to think for yourself. You feel him around you and behind you and beside you every minute, and you keep wondering not what you really feel about anything, but what John Mark wants you to feel. Ain't that the straight of it?"

She glanced apprehensively at John Mark, and, seeing that he did not move to resent this assertion, she looked again with wide-eyed wonder at Ronicky Doone.

"You see," said the man of the sneer to Caroline Smith, "that our friend from the West has a child-like faith in my powers of—what shall I say—hypnotism!"

A faint smile of agreement flickered on her lips and went out. Then she regarded Ronicky, with an utter lack of emotion.

"If I could talk like him," said Ronicky Doone

121

gravely, "I sure wouldn't care where I had to do the talking; but I haven't any smooth lingo—I ain't got a lot of words all ready and handy. I'm a pretty simple-minded sort of a gent, Miss Smith. That's why I want to get you out of this house, where I can talk to you alone."

She paused, then shook her head.

"As far as going out with me goes," went on Ronicky, "well, they's nothing I can say except to ask you to look at me close, lady, and then ask yourself if I'm the sort of a gent a girl has got anything to be afraid about. I won't keep you long; five minutes is all I ask. And we can walk up and down the street, in plain view of the house, if you want. Is it a go?"

At least he had broken through the surface crust of indifference. She was looking at him now, with a shade of interest and sympathy, but she shook her head.

"I'm afraid—" she began.

"Don't refuse right off, without thinking," said Ronicky. "I've worked pretty hard to get a chance to meet you, face to face. I busted into this house tonight like a burglar—"

"Oh," cried the girl, "you're the man—Harry Morgan—" She stopped, aghast.

"He's the man who nearly killed Morgan," said John Mark.

"Is that against me?" asked Ronicky eagerly. "Is that all against me? I was fighting for the chance to find you and talk to you. Give me that chance now."

Obviously she could not make up her mind. It had been curious that this handsome, boyish fellow should come as an emissary from Bill Gregg. It was more curious still that he should have had the daring and the strength to beat Harry Morgan.

"What shall I do, Ruth?" she asked suddenly.

Ruth Tolliver glanced apprehensively at John Mark and then flushed, but she raised her head bravely. "If I were you, Caroline," she said steadily, "I'd simply ask myself if I could trust Ronicky Doone. Can you?"

The girl faced Ronicky again, her hands clasped in indecision and excitement. Certainly, if clean honesty was ever written in the face of a man, it stood written in the clear-cut features of Ronicky Doone.

"Yes," she said at last, "I'll go. For five minutes—only in the street—in full view of the house."

There was a hard, deep-throated exclamation from John Mark. He rose and glided across the room, as if to go and vent his anger elsewhere. But he checked and controlled himself at the door, then turned.

"You seem to have won, Doone. I congratulate you. When he's talking to you, Caroline, I want you constantly to remember that—"

"Wait!" cut in Ronicky sharply. "She'll do her own thinking, without your help."

John Mark bowed with a sardonic smile, but his face was colorless. Plainly he had been hard hit. "Later on," he continued, "we'll see more of each other, I expect—a great deal more, Doone."

"It's something I'll sure wait for," said Ronicky savagely. "I got more than one little thing to talk over with you, Mark. Maybe about some of them we'll have to do more than talking. Goodby. Lady, I'll be waiting for you down by the front door of the house."

Caroline Smith nodded, flung one frightened and appealing glance to Ruth Tolliver for direction, then hurried out to her room to dress. Ronicky Doone turned back to Ruth.

"In my part of the country," he said simply, "they's some gents we know sort of casual, and some gents we have for friends. Once in a while you bump into somebody that's so straight and square-shooting that you'd like to have him for a partner. If you were out West, lady, and if you were a man—well, I'd pick you for a partner, because you've sure played straight and square with me tonight."

He turned, hesitated, and, facing her again, caught up her hand, touched it to his lips, then hurried past John Mark and through the doorway. They could hear his rapid footfalls descending the stairs, and John Mark was thoughtful indeed. He was watching Ruth Tolliver, as she stared down at her hand. When she raised her head and met the glance of the leader she flushed slowly to the roots of her hair.

"Yes," muttered John Mark, still thoughtfully and half to himself, "there's really true steel in him. He's done more against me in one half hour than any other dozen men in ten years."

Chapter Fourteen

Her Little Joke

A brief ten minutes of waiting beside the front door of the house, and then Ronicky Doone heard a swift pattering of feet on the stairs. Presently the girl was moving very slowly toward him down the hall. Plainly she was bitterly afraid when she came beside him, under the dim hall light. She wore that same black hat, turned back from her white face, and the red flower beside it was a dull, uncertain blur. Decidedly she was pretty enough to explain Bill Gregg's sorrow.

Ronicky gave her no chance to think twice. She was in the very act of murmuring something about a change of mind, when he opened the door and, stepping out into the starlight, invited her with a smile and a gesture to follow.

In a moment they were in the freshness of the night air. He took her arm, and they passed slowly down the steps. At the bottom she turned and looked anxiously at the house.

"Lady," murmured Ronicky, "they's nothing to be afraid of. We're going to walk right up and down this street and never get out of sight of the friends you got in this here house."

At the word "friends" she shivered slightly, and he added: "Unless you want to go farther of your own free will."

"No, no!" she exclaimed, as if frightened by the very prospect.

"Then we won't. It's all up to you. You're the boss, and I'm the cow-puncher, lady."

"But tell me quickly," she urged. "I—I have to go back. I mustn't stay out too long."

"Starting right in at the first," Ronicky said, "I got to tell you that Bill has told me pretty much everything that ever went on between you two. All about the correspondence-school work and about the letters and about the pictures."

"I don't understand," murmured the girl faintly.

But Ronicky diplomatically raised his voice and went on, as if he had not heard her. "You know what he's done with that picture of yours?"

"No," she said faintly.

"He got the biggest nugget that he's ever taken out of the dirt. He got it beaten out into the right shape, and then he made a locket out of it and put your picture in it, and now he wears it around his neck, even when he's working at the mine."

Her breath caught. "That silly, cheap snapshot!"

She stopped. She had admitted everything already, and she had intended to be a very sphinx with this strange Westerner.

"It was only a joke," she said. "I—I didn't really mean to—"

"Do you know what that joke did?" asked Ronicky. "It made two men fight, then cross the continent together and get on the trail of a girl whose name they didn't even know. They found the girl, and then she said she'd forgotten—but no, I don't mean to blame you. There's something queer behind it all. But I want to explain one thing. The reason that Bill didn't get to that train wasn't because he didn't try. He did try. He tried so hard that he got into a fight with a gent that tried to hold him up for a few words, and Bill got shot off his hoss."

"Shot?" asked the girl. "Shot?"

Suddenly she was clutching his arm, terrified at the thought. She recovered herself at once and drew away, eluding the hand of Ronicky. He made no further attempt to detain her.

But he had lifted the mask and seen the real state of her mind; and she, too, knew that the secret was discovered. It angered her and threw her instantly on the aggressive.

"I tell you what I guessed from the window," said Ronicky. "You went down to the street, all prepared to meet up with poor old Bill—"

"Prepared to meet him?" She started up at Ronicky. "How in the world could I ever guess—"

She was looking up to him, trying to drag his eyes down to hers, but Ronicky diplomatically kept his attention straight ahead.

"You couldn't guess," he suggested, "but there was someone who could guess for you. Someone who pretty well knew we were in town, who wanted to keep you away from Bill because he was afraid—"

"Of what?" she demanded sharply.

"Afraid of losing you."

This seemed to frighten her. "What do you know?" she asked.

"I know this," he answered, "that I think a girl like you, all in all, is too good for any man. But, if any man ought to have her, it's the gent that is fondest of her. And Bill is terrible fond of you, lady—he don't think of nothing else. He's grown thin as a ghost, longing for you."

"So he sends another man to risk his life to find me and tell me about it?" she demanded, between anger and sadness.

"He didn't send me—I just came. But the reason I came was because I knew Bill would give up without a fight."

"I hate a man who won't fight," said the girl.

"It's because he figures he's so much beneath you," said Ronicky. "And, besides, he can't talk about himself. He's no good at that at all. But, if it comes to fighting, lady, why, he rode a couple of hosses to death and stole another and had a gunfight, all for the sake of seeing you, when a train passed through a town."

She was speechless.

"So I thought I'd come," said Ronicky Doone, "and tell you the insides of things, the way I knew Bill wouldn't and couldn't, but I figure it don't mean nothing much to you."

She did not answer directly. She only said: "Are men like this in the West? Do they do so much for their friends?"

"For a gent like Bill Gregg, that's simple and straight from the shoulder, they ain't nothing too good to be done for him. What I'd do for him he'd do mighty pronto for me, and what he'd do for me—well, don't you figure that he'd do ten times as much for the girl he loves? Be honest with me," said Ronicky Doone. "Tell me if Bill means anymore to you than any stranger?"

"No—yes."

"Which means simply yes. But how much more, lady?"

"I hardly know him. How can I say?"

"It's sure an easy thing to say. You've wrote to him. You've had letters from him. You've sent him your picture, and he's sent you his, and you've seen him on the street. Lady, you sure know Bill Gregg, and what do you think of him?"

"I think—"

"Is he a square sort of gent?"

"Y-yes."

"The kind you'd trust?"

"Yes, but—"

"Is he the kind that would stick to the girl he loved and take care of her, through thick and thin?"

"You mustn't talk like this," said Caroline Smith, but her voice trembled, and her eyes told him to go on.

"I'm going back and tell Bill Gregg that, down in your heart, you love him just about the same as he loves you!"

"Oh," she asked, "would you say a thing like that? It isn't a bit true."

"I'm afraid that's the way I see it. When I tell him that, you can lay to it that old Bill will let loose all holds and start for you, and, if they's ten brick walls and twenty gunmen in between, it won't make no difference. He'll find you, or die trying."

Before he finished she was clinging to his arm.

"If you tell him, you'll be doing a murder, Ronicky Doone. What he'll face will be worse than twenty gunmen."

"The gent that smiles, eh?"

"Yes, John Mark. No, no, I didn't mean—"

"But you did, and I knew it, too. It's John Mark that's between you and Bill. I seen you in the street, when you were talking to poor Bill, look back over your shoulder at that devil standing in the window of this house."

"Don't call him that!"

"D'you know of one drop of kindness in his nature, lady?"

"Are we quite alone?"

"Not a soul around."

"Then he is a devil, and, being a devil, no ordinary man has a chance against him—not a chance, Ronicky Doone. I don't know what you did in the house, but I think you must have outfaced him in some way. Well, for that you'll pay, be sure! And you'll pay with your life, Ronicky. Every minute, now, you're in danger of your life. You'll keep on being in danger, until he feels that he has squared his account with you. Don't you see that if I let Bill Gregg come near me—"

"Then Bill will be in danger of this same wolf of a man, eh? And, in spite of the fact that you like Bill—"

"Ah, yes, I do!"

"That you love him, in fact."

"Why shouldn't I tell you?" demanded the girl, breaking down suddenly. "I do love him, and I can never see him to tell him, because I dread John Mark."

"Rest easy," said Ronicky, "you'll see Bill, or else he'll die trying to get to you."

"If you're his friend—"

"I'd rather see him dead than living the rest of his life, plumb unhappy."

She shook her head, arguing, and so they reached the corner of Beekman Place again and turned into it and went straight toward the house opposite that of John Mark. Still the girl argued, but it was in a whisper, as if she feared that terrible John Mark might overhear.

*   *   *

In the home of John Mark, that calm leader was still with Ruth Tolliver. They had gone down to the lower floor of the house, and, at his request, she sat at the piano, while Mark sat comfortably beyond the sphere of the piano light and watched her.

"You're thinking of something else," he told her, "and playing abominably."

"I'm sorry."

"You ought to be," he said. "It's bad enough to play poorly for someone who doesn't know, but it's torture to play like that for me."

He spoke without violence, as always, but she knew that he was intensely angry, and that familiar chill passed through her body. It never failed to come when she felt that she had aroused his anger.

"Why doesn't Caroline come back?" she asked at length.

"She's letting him talk himself out, that's all. Caroline's a clever youngster. She knows how to let a man talk till his throat is dry, and then she'll smile and tell him that it's impossible to agree with him. Yes, there are many possibilities in Caroline."

"You think Ronicky Doone is a gambler?" she asked, harking back to what he had said earlier.

"I think so," answered John Mark, and again there was that tightening of the muscles around his mouth. "A gambler has a certain way of masking his own face and looking at yours, as if he were dragging your thoughts out through your eyes; also, he's very cool; he belongs at a table with the cards on it and the stakes high."

The door opened. "Here's young Rose. He'll tell us the truth of the matter. Has she come back, Rose?"

The young fellow kept far back in the shadow, and, when he spoke, his voice was uncertain, almost to the point of trembling. "No," he managed to say, "she ain't come back, chief."

Mark stared at him for a moment and then slowly opened a cigarette case and lighted a smoke. "Well," he said, and his words were far more violent than the smooth voice, "well, idiot, what did she do?"

"She done a fade-away, chief, in the house across the street. Went in with that other gent."

"He took her by force?" asked John Mark.

"Nope. She slipped in quick enough and all by herself. He went in last."

"Damnation!" murmured Mark. "That's all, Rose."

His follower vanished through the doorway and closed the door softly after him. John Mark stood up and paced quietly up and down the room. At length he turned abruptly on the girl. "Good night. I have business that takes me out."

"What is it?" she asked eagerly.

He paused, as if in doubt as to how he should answer her, if he answered at all. "In the old days," he said at last, "when a man caught a poacher on his grounds, do you know what he did?"

"No."

"Shot him, my dear, without a thought and threw his body to the wolves!"

"John Mark! Do you mean—"

"Your friend Ronicky, of course."

"Only because Caroline was foolish are you going to—"

"Caroline? Tut, tut! Caroline is only a small part of it. He has done more than that—far more, this poacher out of the West!"

He turned and went swiftly through the door. The moment it was closed the girl buried her face in her hands.

Chapter Fifteen

The Girl Thief

Before that death sentence had been passed on him Ronicky Doone stood before the door of his room, with the trembling girl beside him.

"Wait here," he whispered to her. "Wait here while I go in and wake him up. It's going to be the greatest moment in his life! Poor Bill Gregg is going to turn into the richest man in New York City—all in one moment!"

"But I don't dare go in. It will mean—"

"It will mean everything, but it's too late to turn back now. Besides, in your heart of hearts, you don't want to turn back, you know!"

Quickly he passed into the room and hurried to the bed of Bill Gregg. Under the biting grip of Doone's hand Bill Gregg writhed to a sitting posture, with a groan. Still he was in the throes of his dream and only half awakened.

"I've lost her," he whispered.

"You're wrong, idiot," said Ronicky softly, "you're wrong. You've won her. She's at the door now, waiting to come in."

"Ronicky," said Bill Gregg, suddenly awake, "you've been the finest friend a man ever had, but, if you make a joke out of her, I'll wring your neck!"

"Sure you would. But, before you do that, jump into your clothes and open the door."

Sleep was still thick enough in the brain of Bill Gregg to make him obey automatically. He stumbled into his clothes and then shambled dizzily to the door and opened it. As the light from the room struck down the hall Ronicky saw his friend stiffen to his full height and strike a hand across his face.

"Stars and Stripes!" exclaimed Bill Gregg. "The days of the miracles ain't over!"

Ronicky Doone turned his back and went to the window. Across the street rose the forbidding face of the house of John Mark, and it threatened Ronicky Doone like a clenched hand, brandished against him. The shadow under the upper gable was like the shadow under a frowning brow. In that house worked the mind of John Mark. Certainly Ronicky Doone had won the first stage of the battle between them, but there was more to come—much more of that battle—and who would win in the end was an open question. He made up his mind grimly that, whatever happened, he would first ship Bill Gregg and the girl out of the city, then act as the rear guard to cover their retreat.

When he returned they had closed the door and were standing back from one another, with such shining eyes that the heart of Ronicky Doone leaped. If, for a moment, doubt of his work came to him, it was banished, as they glanced toward him.

"I dunno how he did it," Bill Gregg was stammering, "but here it is—done! Bless you, Ronicky."

"A minute ago," said Ronicky, "it looked to me like the lady didn't know her own mind, but that seems to be over."

"I found my own mind the moment I saw him," said the girl.

Ronicky studied her in wonder. There was no embarrassment, no shame to have confessed herself. She had the clear brow of a child. Suddenly, it seemed to Ronicky that he had become an old man, and these were two children under his protection. He struck into the heart of the problem at once.

"The main point," he said, "is to get you two out of town, as quick as we can. Out West in Bill's country he can take care of you, but back here this John Mark is a devil and has the strength to stop us. How quick can you go, Caroline?"

"I can never go," she said, "as long as John Mark is alive."

"Then he's as good as dead," said Bill Gregg. "We both got guns, and, no matter how husky

John Mark may be, we'll get at him!"

The girl shook her head. All the joy had gone out of her face and left her wistful and misty eyed. "You don't understand, and I can't tell you. You can never harm John Mark."

"Why not?" asked Bill Gregg. "Has he got a thousand men around him all the time? Even if he has they's ways of getting at him."

"Not a thousand men," said the girl, "but, you see, he doesn't need help. He's never failed. That's what they say of him: 'John Mark, the man who has never lost!'"

"Listen to me," said Ronicky angrily. "Seems to me that everybody stands around and gapes at this gent with the sneer a terrible lot, without a pile of good reasons behind 'em. Never failed? Why, lady, here's one night when he's failed and failed bad. He's lost you!"

"No," said Caroline.

"Not lost you?" asked Bill Gregg. "Say, you ain't figuring on going back to him?"

"I have to go back."

"Why?" demanded Gregg.

"It's because of you," interpreted Ronicky Doone. "She knows that, if she leaves you, Mark will start on your trail. Mark is the name of the gent with the sneer, Bill."

"He's got to die, then, Ronicky."

"I been figuring on the same thing for a long time, but he'll die hard, Bill."

"Don't you see?" asked the girl. "Both of you are strong men and brave, but against John Mark I know that you're helpless. It isn't the first time people have hated him. Hated? Who does anything but hate him? But that doesn't make any difference. He wins, he always wins, and that's why I've come to you."

She turned to Bill Gregg, but such a sad resignation held her eyes that Ronicky Doone bowed his head.

"I've come to tell you that I love you, that I have always loved you, since I first began writing to you. All of yourself showed through your letters, plain and strong and simple and true. I've come tonight to tell you that I love you, but that we can never marry. Not that I fear him for myself, but for you."

"Listen here," said Bill Gregg, "ain't there police in this town?"

"What could they do? In all of the things which he has done no one has been able to accuse him of a single illegal act—at least no one has ever been able to prove a thing. And yet he lives by crime. Does that give you an idea of the sort of man he is?"

"A low hound," said Bill Gregg bitterly, "that's what he shows to be."

"Tell me straight," said Ronicky, "what sort of a hold has he got over you? Can you tell us?"

"I have to tell you," said the girl gravely, "if you insist, but won't you take my word for it and ask no more?"

"We have a right to know," said Ronicky. "Bill has a right, and, me being Bill's friend, I have a right, too."

She nodded.

"First off, what's the way John Mark uses you?"

She clenched her hands. "If I tell you that, you will both despise me."

"Try us," said Ronicky. "And you can lay to this, lady, that, when a gent out of the West says 'partner' to a girl or a man, he means it. What you do may be bad; what you are is all right. We both know it. The inside of you is right, lady, no matter what John Mark makes you do. But tell us straight, what is it?"

"He has made me," said the girl, her head falling, "a thief!"

Ronicky saw Bill Gregg wince, as if someone had struck him in the face. And he himself waited, curious to see what the big fellow would do. He had not long to wait. Gregg went straight to the girl and took her hands.

"D'you think that makes any difference?" he asked. "Not to me, and not to my friend Ronicky. There's something behind it. Tell us that!"

"There is something behind it," said the girl, "and I can't say how grateful I am to you both for still trusting me. I have a brother. He came to New York to work, found it was easy to spend money—and spent it. Finally he began sending home for money. We are not rich, but we gave him what we could. It went on like that for some time. Then, one day, a stranger called at our house, and it was John Mark. He wanted to see me, and, when we talked together, he told me that my brother had done a terrible thing— what it was I can't tell even you.

"I wouldn't believe at first, though he showed me what looked like proofs. At last I believed enough to agree to go to New York and see for myself. I came here, and saw my brother and made him confess. What it was I can't tell you. I can only say that his life is in the hand of John Mark. John Mark has only to say ten words, and my brother is dead. He told me that. He showed me the hold that Mark had over him, and begged me to do what I could for him. I didn't see how I could be of use to him, but John Mark showed me. He taught me to steal, and I have stolen. He taught me to lie, and I have lied. And he has me still in the hollow of his hand, do you see? And that's why I say that it's hopeless. Even if you could fight against John Mark, which no one can, you couldn't help me. The moment you strike him he strikes my brother."

"Curse him!" exclaimed Ronicky. "Curse the hound!" Then he added: "They's just one thing to do, first of all. You got to go back to John Mark. Tell him that you came over here. Tell him that you seen Bill Gregg, but you only came to say good-by to him, and to ask him to leave town and go West. Then, tomorrow, we'll move out, and he may think that we've gone. Meantime the thing you do is to give me the name of your brother and tell me where I can find him. I'll hunt him up. Maybe something can be done for him. I dunno, but that's where we've got to try."

"But—" she began.

"Do what he says," whispered Bill Gregg. "I've

doubted Ronicky before, but look at all that he's done? Do what he says, Caroline."

"It means putting him in your power," she said at last, "just as he was put in the power of John Mark, but I trust you. Give me a slip of paper, and I'll write on it what you want."

Chapter Sixteen

Disarming Suspicion

From the house across the street Caroline Smith slipped out upon the pavement and glanced warily about her. The street was empty, quieter and more villagelike than ever, yet she knew perfectly well that John Mark had not allowed her to be gone so long without keeping watch over her. Somewhere from the blank faces of those houses across the street his spies kept guard over her movements. Here she glanced sharply over her shoulder, and it seemed to her that a shadow flitted into the door of a basement, farther up the street.

At that she fled and did not stop running until she was at the door of the house of Mark. Since all was quiet, up and down the street, she paused again, her hand upon the knob. To enter meant to step back into the life which she hated. There had been a time when she had almost loved the life to which John Mark introduced her; there had been a time when she had rejoiced in the nimbleness of her fingers which had enabled her to become an adept as a thief. And, by so doing, she had kept the life of her brother from danger, she verily believed. She was still saving him, and, so long as she worked for John Mark, she knew that her brother was safe, yet she hesitated long at the door.

It would be only the work of a moment to flee back to the man she loved, tell him that she could not and dared not stay longer with the master criminal, and beg him to take her West to a clean life. Her hand fell from the knob, but she raised it again immediately.

It would not do to flee, so long as John Mark had power of life or death over her brother. If Ronicky Doone, as he promised, was able to inspire her brother with the courage to flee from New York, give up his sporting life and seek refuge in some far-off place, then, indeed, she would go with Bill Gregg to the ends of the earth and mock the cunning fiend who had controlled her life so long.

The important thing now was to disarm him of all suspicion, make him feel that she had only visited Bill Gregg in order to say farewell to him. With this in her mind she opened the front door and stepped into the hall, always lighted with ominous dimness. That gloom fell about her like the visible presence of John Mark.

A squat, powerful figure glided out of the door-way to the right. It was Harry Morgan, and the side of his face was swathed in bandages, so that he had to twist his mouth violently in order to speak.

"The chief," he said abruptly. "Beat it quick to his room. He wants you."

"Why?" asked Caroline, hoping to extract some grain or two of information from the henchman.

"Listen, kid," said the sullen criminal. "D'you think I'm a nut to blow what I know? You beat it, and he'll tell you what he wants."

The violence of this language, however, had given her clues enough to the workings of the chief's mind. She had always been a favored member of the gang, and the men had whis-tled attendance on her hardly less than upon Ruth Tolliver herself. This sudden harshness in the language of Harry Morgan told her that too much was known, or guessed.

A sudden weakness came over her. "I'm going out," she said, turning to Harry Morgan who had sauntered over to the front door.

"Are you?" he asked.

"I'm going to take one turn more up the block. I'm not sleepy yet," she repeated and put her hand on the knob of the door.

"Not so you could notice it, you ain't," retorted Morgan. "We've taken lip enough from you, kid. Your day's over. Go up and see what the chief has to say, but you ain't going through this door unless you walk over me."

"Those are orders?" she asked, stepping back, with her heart turning cold.

"Think I'm doing this on my own hook?"

She turned slowly to the stairs. With her hand on the balustrade she decided to try the effect of one personal appeal. Nerving herself she whirled and ran to Harry Morgan. "Harry," she whispered, "let me go out till I've worked up my courage. You know he's terrible to face when he's angry. And I'm afraid, Harry—I'm terribly afraid!"

"Are you?" asked Morgan. "Well, you ain't the first. Go and take your medicine like the rest of us have done, time and time running."

There was no help for it. She went wearily up the stairs to the room of the master thief. There she gave the accustomed rap with the proper intervals. Instantly the cold, soft voice, which she knew and hated so, called to her to enter.

She found him in the act of putting aside his book. He was seated in a deep easy-chair; a dressing gown of silk and a pair of horn-rimmed spectacles gave him a look of owlish wisdom, with a touch of the owl's futility of expression, likewise. He rose, as usual, with all his courtesy. She thought at first, as he showed her to a chair, that he was going to take his usual damnable tack of pretended ignorance in order to see how much she would confess. However, tonight this was not his plan of battle.

The moment she was seated, he removed his spectacles, drew a chair close to hers and sat down, leaning far forward. "Now, my dear, foolish girl," said the master thief, smiling benevolently upon her, "what have you been doing tonight to make us all miserable?"

She knew at once that he was aware of every move she had made, from the first to the last. It gave her firmness to tell the lie with suavity. "It's a queer yarn, John," she said.

"I'm used to queer yarns," he answered. "But where have you been all this time? It was only to take five minutes, I thought."

She made herself laugh. "That's because you don't know Ronicky Doone, John."

"I'm getting to know him, however," said the master. "And, before I'm done, I hope to know him very well indeed."

"Well, he has a persuasive tongue."

"I think I noticed that for myself."

"And, when he told me how poor Bill Gregg had come clear across the continent—"

"No wonder you were touched, my dear. New Yorkers won't travel so far, will they? Not for a girl, I mean."

"Hardly! But Ronicky Doone made it such a sad affair that I promised I'd go across and see Bill Gregg."

"Not in his room?"

"I knew you wouldn't let him come to see me here."

"Never presuppose what I'll do. But go on—I'm interested—very. Just as much as if Ronicky Doone himself were telling me."

She eyed him shrewdly, but, if there were any

deception in him, he hid it well. She could not find the double meaning that must have been behind his words. "I went there, however," she said, "because I was sorry for him, John. If you had seen you'd have been sorry, too, or else you would have laughed; I could hardly keep from it at first."

"I suppose he took you in his arms at once?"

"I think he wanted to. Then, of course, I told him at once why I had come."

"Which was?"

"Simply that it was absurd for him to stay about and persecute me; that the letters I wrote him were simply written for fun, when I was doing some of my cousin's work at the correspondence schools; that the best thing he could do would be to take my regrets and go back to the West."

"Did you tell him all that?" asked John Mark in a rather changed voice.

"Yes; but not quite so bluntly."

"Naturally not; you're a gentle girl, Caroline. I suppose he took it very hard."

"Very, but in a silly way. He's full of pride, you see. He drew himself up and gave me a lecture about deceiving men."

"Well, since you have lost interest in him, it makes no difference."

"But in a way," she said faintly, rising slowly from her chair, "I can't help feeling some interest."

"Naturally not. But, you see, I was worried so much about you and this foolish fellow that I gave orders for him to be put out of the way, as soon as you left him."

Caroline Smith stood for a moment stunned and then ran to him.

"No, no!" she declared. "In the name of the dear mercy of Heaven, John, you haven't done that?"

"I'm sorry."

"Then call him back—the one you sent. Call him back, John, and I'll serve you the rest of my life without question. I'll never fail you, John, but for your own sake and mine, for the sake of everything fair in the world, call him back!"

He pushed away her hands, but without violence. "I thought it would be this way," he said coldly. "You told a very good lie, Caroline. I suppose clever Ronicky Doone rehearsed you in it, but it needed only the oldest trick in the world to expose you."

She recoiled from him. "It was only a joke, then? You didn't mean it, John? Thank Heaven for that!"

A savagery which, though generally concealed, was never far from the surface, now broke out in him, making the muscles of his face tense and his voice metallic. "Get to your room," he said fiercely, "get to your room. I've wasted time enough on you and your brat of a brother, and now a Western lout is to spoil what I've done? I've a mind to wash my hands of all of you—and sink you. Get to your room, and stay there, while I make up my mind which of the two I shall do."

She went, cringing like one beaten, to the door, and he followed her, trembling with rage.

"Or have you a choice?" he asked. "Brother or lover, which shall it be?"

She turned and stretched out her hands to him, unable to speak; but the man of the sneer struck down her arms and laughed in her face. In mute terror she fled to her room.

Chapter Seventeen

Old Scars

In his room Bill Gregg was striding up and down, throwing his hands toward the ceiling. Now and then he paused to slap Ronicky Doone on the back.

"It's fate, Ronicky," he said, over and over again. "Thinking of waking up and finding the girl that you've loved and lost standing waiting for you! It's the dead come to life. I'm the happiest man in the world. Ronicky, old boy, one of these days I'll be able—" He paused, stopped by the solemnity of Doone's face. "What's wrong, Ronicky?"

"I don't know," said the other gloomily. He rubbed his arms slowly, as if to bring back the circulation to numbed limbs.

"You act like you're sick, Ronicky."

"I'm getting bad-luck signs, Bill. That's the short of it."

"How come?"

"The old scars are prickling."

"Scars? What scars?"

"Ain't you noticed 'em."

It was bedtime, so Ronicky Doone took off his coat and shirt. The rounded body, alive with playing muscles, was striped, here and there, with white streaks—scars left by healed wounds.

"At your age? A kid like you with scars?" Bill Gregg had been asking, and then he saw the exposed scars and gasped. "How come, Ronicky," he asked huskily in his astonishment, "that you got all those and ain't dead yet?"

"I dunno," said the other. "I wonder a pile about that, myself. Fact is I'm a lucky gent, Bill Gregg."

"They say back yonder in your country that you ain't never been beaten, Ronicky."

"They sure say a lot of foolish things, just to hear themselves talk, partner. A gent gets pretty good with a gun, then they say he's the best that ever breathed—that he's never been beat. But they forget things that happened just a year back. No, sir; I sure took my lickings when I started."

"But, dog-gone it, Ronicky, you ain't twenty-four now!"

"Between sixteen and twenty-two I spent a pile of time in bed, Bill, and you can lay to that!"

"And you kept practicing?"

"Sure, when I found out that I had to. I never liked shooting much. Hated to think of having a gent's life right inside the crook of my trigger finger. But, when I seen that I had to get good, why I just let go all holds and practiced day and night. And I still got to practice."

"I seen that," said Bill Gregg. "Every day, for an hour or two, you work with your guns."

"It's like being a musician," said Ronicky without enthusiasm. "I heard about it once. Suppose a gent works up to be a fine musician, maybe at the piano. You'd think, when he got to the top and knew everything, he could lay off and take things easy the rest of his life. But not him! Nope, he's got to work like a slave every day."

"But how come you felt them scars pricking as a bad-luck sign, Ronicky?" he asked after a time. "Is there anything that's gone wrong, far as you see?"

"I dunno," said Ronicky gravely. "Maybe not, and maybe so. I ain't a prophet, but I don't like having everything so smooth—not when they's a gent like the man with the sneer on the other end of the wire. It means he's holding back some cards on us, and I'd sure like to see the color of what he's got. What I'm going to work for is this, Bill: To get Caroline's brother, Jerry Smith, and rustle him out of town."

"But how can you do that when John Mark has a hold on him?"

"That's a pile of bunk, Bill. I figure Mark is just bluffing. He ain't going to turn anybody over to the police. Less he has to do with the police the happier he'll be. You can lay to that. Matter of fact, he's been loaning money to Caroline's brother. You heard her say that. Also, he thinks that Mark is the finest and most generous gent that ever stepped. Probably a selfish skunk of a spoiled kid, this brother of hers. Most like he puts Mark up as sort of an ideal. Well, the thing to do is to get hold of him and wake him up and pay off his debts to Mark, which most like run to several thousand."

"Several thousand, Ronicky? But where'll we get the money?"

"You forget that I can always get money. It grows on the bushes for me." He grinned at Bill Gregg.

"Once we get Jerry Smith, then the whole gang of us will head straight West, as fast as we can step. Now let's hit the hay."

Never had the mind of Ronicky Doone worked more quickly and surely to the point. The case of Jerry Smith was exactly what he had surmised. As for the crime of which John Mark knew, and which he held like a club over Jerry Smith, it had been purely and simply an act of self-defense. But, to Caroline and her brother, Mark had made it seem clear that the shadow of the electric chair was before the young fellow.

Mark had worked seriously to win Caroline. She was remarkably dexterous; she was the soul of courage; and, if he could once make her love her work, she would make him rich.

In the meantime she did very well indeed, and he strengthened his hold on her through her brother. It was not hard to do. If Jerry Smith was the soul of recklessness, he was the soul of honor, also, in many ways. John Mark had only to lead the boy toward a life of heavy expenditures and gaming, lending him, from time to time, the wherewithal to keep it up. In this way he anchored Jerry as a safeguard to windward, in case of trouble.

But, now that Ronicky Doone had entered the tangle, everything was changed. That clear-eyed fellow might see through to the very bottom of Mark's tidewater plans. He might step in and cut the Gordian knot by simply paying off Jerry's debts. Telling the boy to laugh at the danger of exposure, Doone could snatch him away to the West. So Mark came to forestall Ronicky, by sending Jerry out of town and out of reach, for the time being. He would not risk the effect of Ronicky's tongue. Had not Caroline been persuaded under his very eyes by this strange Westerner?

Very early the next morning John Mark went straight to the apartment of his protégé. It was his own man, Northup, who answered the bell and opened the door to him. He had supplied Northup to Jerry Smith, immediately after Caroline accomplished the lifting of the Larrigan emeralds. That clever piece of work had proved the worth of the girl and made it necessary to spare no expense on Jerry.

So he had given him the tried and proven Northup.

The moment he looked into the grinning face of Northup he knew that the master was not at home, and both the chief and the servant relaxed. They were friends of too long a term to stand on ceremony.

"There's no one here?" asked Mark, as a matter of form.

"Not a soul—the kid skipped—not a soul in the house."

"Suppose he were to come up behind the door and hear you talk about him like this, Northup? He's trim you down nicely, eh?"

"Him?" asked Northup, with an eloquent jerk of his hand. "He's a husky young brute, but it ain't brute force that I work with." He smiled significantly into the face of the other, and John Mark smiled in return. They understood one another perfectly.

"When is he coming back?"

"Didn't leave any word, chief."

"Isn't this earlier than his usual time for starting the day?"

"It is, by five hours. The lazy pup don't usually crack an eye till one in the afternoon."

"What happened this morning."

"Something rare—something it would have done your heart good to see!"

"Out with it, Northup."

"I was routed out of bed at eight by a jangling of the telephone. The operator downstairs said a gentleman was calling on Mr. Smith. I said, of course, that Mr. Smith couldn't be called on at that hour. Then the operator said the gentleman would come up to the door and explain. I told him to come ahead.

"At the door of the apartment I met as fine looking a youngster as I ever laid eyes on, brown as a berry, with a quick, straight look about the eyes that would have done you good to see. No booze or dope in that face, chief. He said—"

"How tall was he?" asked the chief.

"About my height. Know him?"

"Maybe. What name did he give?"

"Didn't give a name. 'I've come to surprise Jerry,' he says to me.

"'Anybody would surprise Jerry at this hour of the morning,'" says I.

"'It's too early, I take it?' says he.

"'About five hours,' says I.

"'Then this is going to be one of the exceptions,' says he.

"'If you knew Jerry better you wouldn't force yourself on him,' says I.

"'Son,' says this fresh kid—"

"Is this the way you talk to Smith?" broke in Mark.

"No, I can polish up my lingo with the best of 'em. But this brown-faced youngster was a card. 'Son,' he says to me, 'I'll do my own explaining. Just lead me to his dugout.'

"I couldn't help laughing. 'You'll get a hot reception,' says I.

"'I come from a hot country,' says he, 'and I got no doubt that Jerry will try to make me at home,' and he grinned with a devil in each eye.

"'Come in, then,' says I, and in he steps. 'And mind your fists,' says I, 'if you wake him up sudden. He fights sometimes because he has to, but mostly because it's a pleasure to him.'

"'Sure,' says he. 'That's the way I like to have 'em come.'"

"And he went in?" demanded John Mark.

"What's wrong with that?" asked Northup anxiously.

"Nothing. Go ahead."

"Well, in he went to Jerry's room. I listened at the door. I heard him call Jerry, and then Jerry groaned like he was half dead.

"'I don't know you,' says Jerry.

"'You will before I'm through with you,' says the other.

"'Who the devil are you?' asks Jerry.

"'Doone is my name,' says he.

"'Then go to the devil till one o'clock,' says Jerry. 'And come back then if you want to. Here's my time for a beauty sleep.'

"'If it's that time,' says Doone, 'you'll have to go ugly today. I'm here to talk.'

"I heard Jerry sit up in bed.

"'Now what the devil's the meaning of this?' he asked.

"'Are you awake?' says Doone.

"'Yes, but be hung to you!' says Jerry.

"Don't be hanging me,' says Doone. 'You just mark this day down in red—it's a lucky one for you, son.'

" 'An' how d'you mean that?' says Jerry, and I could hear by his voice that he was choking, he was that crazy mad.

" 'Because it's the day you met me,' says Doone; 'that's why it's a lucky one for you.'

" 'Listen to me,' says Jerry, 'of all the nervy, cold-blooded fakers that ever stepped you're the nerviest.'

" 'Thanks,' says Doone. 'I think I am doing pretty well.'

" 'If I wanted to waste the time,' says Jerry, 'I'd get up and throw you out.'

" 'It's a wise man,' says Doone, 'that does his talking from the other side of a rock.'

" 'Well,' says Jerry, 'd'you think I can't throw you out?'

" 'Anyway,' says Doone, 'I'm still here.'

"I heard the springs squeal, as Jerry went bouncing out of bed. For a minute they wrestled, and I opened the door. What I see was Jerry lying flat, and Doone sitting on his chest, as calm and smiling as you please. I closed the door quick. Jerry's too game a boy to mind being licked fair and square, but, of course, he'd rather fight till he died than have me or anybody else see him give up.

" 'I dunno how you got there,' says Jerry, 'but, if I don't kill you for this later on, I'd like to shake hands with you. It was a good trick.'

" 'The gent that taught me near busted me in two with the trick of it,' said Doone. 'S'pose I let you up. Is it to be a handshaking or fighting?'

" 'My wind is gone for half an hour,' says Jerry, 'and my head is pretty near jarred loose from my spinal column. I guess it'll have to be hand-shaking today. But I warn you, Doone,' he says, 'someday I'll have it all out with you over again.'

" 'Any time you mention,' says Doone, 'but, if you'd landed that left when you rushed in, I would have been on the carpet, instead of you.'

"And Jerry chuckles, feeling a pile better to think how near he'd come to winning the fight.

" 'Wait till I jump under the shower,' says Jerry, 'and I'll be with you again. Have you had breakfast? And what brought you to me? And who the devil are you, Doone? Are you out of the West?'

"He piles all these questions thick and fast at Doone, and then I seen right off that him and Doone had made up to be pretty thick with each other. So I went away from the door and didn't listen any more, and in about half an hour out they walk, arm in arm, like old pals."

It was perfectly clear to John Mark that Ronicky had come there purposely to break the link between him and young Jerry Smith. It was perfectly plain why he wanted to do it.

"How much does Jerry owe me?" he asked suddenly.

The other drew out a pad and calculated for a moment: "Seven thousand eight hundred and forty-two," he announced with a grin, as he put back the pad. "That's what he's sold himself for, up to this time."

"Too much in a way and not enough in another way," replied John Mark. "Listen, if he comes back, which I doubt, keep him here. Get him away from Ronicky—dope him—dope them both. In any case, if he comes back here, don't let him get away. You understand?"

"Nope, but I don't need to understand. I'll do it."

John Mark nodded and turned toward the door.

Chapter Eighteen

The Spider's Web

Only the select attended the meetings at Fernand's. It was doubly hard to choose them. They had to have enough money to afford high play, and they also had to lose without a murmur. It made it extremely difficult to build up a clientele, but Fernand was equal to the task. He seemed to smell out the character of a man or woman, to know at once how much iron was in their souls. And, following the course of an evening's play, Fernand knew the exact moment at which a man had had enough. It was never twice the same for the same man. A rich fellow, who lost twenty thousand one day and laughed at it, might groan and curse if he lost twenty hundred a week later.

It was Fernand's desire to keep those groans and curses from being heard in his gaming house. He extracted wallets painlessly, so to speak.

He was never crooked; and yet he would not have a dealer in his employ unless the fellow knew every good trick of running up the deck. The reason was that, while Fernand never cheated in order to take money away from his customers, he very, very frequently had his men cheat in order to give money away.

This sounds like a mad procedure for the proprietor of a gaming house, but there were profound reasons beneath it. For one of the maxims of Fernand—and, like every gambler, he had many of them—was that the best way to make a man lose money is first of all to make him win it.

Such was Monsieur Frederic Fernand. And, if many compared him to Falstaff, and many pitied the merry, fat old man for having fallen into so hard a profession, yet there were a few who called him a bloated spider, holding his victims, with invisible cords, and bleeding them slowly to death.

To help him he had selected two men, both young, both shrewd, both iron in will and nerve and courage, both apparently equally expert with the cards, and both just as equally capable of pleasing his clients. One was a Scotchman, McKeever; the other was a Jew, Simonds. But in looks they were as much alike as two peas out of one pod. They hated each other with silent, smiling hatred, because they knew that they were on trial for their fortunes.

Tonight the Jew, Simonds, was dealing at one of the tables, and the Scotchman, McKeever, stood at the side of the master of the house, ready to execute his commissions. Now and again his dark eyes wandered toward the table where the Jew sat, with the cards flashing through his fingers. McKeever hungered to be there on the firing line! How he wished he could feel that sifting of the polished cardboard under his finger tips. They were playing Black Jack. He noted the smooth skill with which Simonds buried a card. And yet the trick was not perfectly done. Had he, McKeever, been there—

At this point he was interrupted by the easy, oily voice of M. Fernand. "This is an infernal nuisance!"

McKeever raised his eyebrows and waited for an explanation. Two young men, very young, very straight, had just come into the rooms. One he knew to be Jerry Smith.

"Another table and dealer wasted," declared M. Fernand. "Smith—and, by heavens, he's brought some friend of his with him!"

"Shall I see if I can turn them away without playing?" asked McKeever.

"No, not yet. Smith is a friend of John Mark. Don't forget that. Never forget, McKeever, that the friends of John Mark must be treated with gloves—always!"

"Very good," replied McKeever, like a pupil memorizing in class.

"I'll see how far I can go with them," went on M. Fernand. He went straight to the telephone and rang John Mark.

"How far should I go with them?" he asked, after he had explained that Smith had just come in.

"Is there someone with him?" asked John Mark eagerly.

"A young chap about the same age—very brown."

"That's the man I want!"

"The man you want?"

"Fernand," said Mark, without explaining, "those youngsters have gone out there to make some money at your expense."

M. Fernand growled. "I wish you'd stop using me as a bank, Mark," he complained. "Besides, it costs a good deal."

"I pay you a tolerable interest, I believe," said John Mark coldly.

"Of course, of course! Well"—this in a manner of great resignation—"how much shall I let them take away?"

"Bleed them both to death if you want. Let them play on credit. Go as far as you like."

"Very well," said Fernand, "but—"

"I may be out there later, myself. Good-by."

The face of Frederic Fernand was dark when he went back to McKeever. "What do you think of the fellow with Jerry Smith?" he asked.

"Of him?" asked McKeever, fencing desperately for another moment, as he stared at Ronicky Doone.

The latter was idling at a table close to the wall, running his hands through a litter of magazines. After a moment he raised his head suddenly and glanced across the room at McKeever. The shock of meeting glances is almost a physical thing. And the bold, calm eyes of Ronicky Doone lingered on McKeever and seemed to judge him and file that judgment away.

McKeever threw himself upon the wings of his imagination. There was something about this fellow, or his opinion would not have been asked. What was it?

"Well?" asked Frederic Fernand peevishly. "What do you think of him?"

"I think," said the other casually, "that he's probably a Western gunman, with a record as long as my arm."

"You think that?" asked the fat man. "Well, I've an idea that you think right. There's something about him that suggests action. The way he looks about, so slowly—that is the way a fearless man is apt to look, you know. Do you think you can sit at the table with Ronicky Doone, as they call him, and Jerry Smith and win from them this evening?"

"With any sort of luck—"

"Leave the luck out of it. John Mark has made a special request. Tonight, McKeever, it's going to be your work to make the luck come to you. Do you think you can?"

A faint smile began to dawn on the face of McKeever. Never in his life had he heard news so sweet to his ear. It meant, in brief, that he was to be trusted for the first time at real manipulation of the cards. His trust in himself was complete. This would be a crushing blow for Simonds.

"Mind you," the master of the house went on, "if you are caught at working—"

"Nonsense!" said McKeever happily. "They can't follow my hands."

"This fellow Doone—I don't know."

"I'll take the chance."

"If you're caught I turn you out. You hear? Are you willing to take the risk?"

"Yes," said McKeever, very pale, but determined.

At the right moment McKeever approached Jerry and Ronicky, dark, handsome, smoothly amiable. He was clever enough to make no indirect effort to introduce his topic. "I see that you gentlemen are looking about," he said. "Yonder is a clear table for us. Do you agree, Mr. Smith?"

Jerry Smith nodded, and, having introduced Ronicky Doone, the three started for the table which had been indicated.

It was in an alcove, apart from the sweep of big rooms which were given over to the players. It lay, too, conveniently in range of the beat of Frederic Fernand, as he moved slowly back and forth, over a limited territory and stopped, here and there for a word, here and there for a smile. He was smoothing the way for dollars to slide out of wallets. Now he deliberately stopped the party in their progress to the alcove.

"I have to meet you," he said to Ronicky. "You remind me of a friend of my father, a young

Westerner, those many years ago. Same brown skin, same clear eye. He was a card expert, the man I'm thinking about. I hope you're not in the same class, my friend!"

Then he went on, laughing thunderously at his own poor jest. Particularly from the back, as he retreated, he seemed a harmless fat man, very simple, very naïve. But Ronicky Doone regarded him with an interest both cold and keen. And, with much the same regard, after Fernand had passed out of view, the Westerner regarded the table at which they were to sit.

In the alcove were three wall lights, giving an ample illumination—too ample to suit Ronicky Doone. For McKeever had taken the chair with the back to the light. He made no comment, but, taking the chair which was facing the lights, the chair which had been pointed out to him by McKeever, he drew it around on the far side and sat down next to the professional gambler.

Chapter Nineteen

Stacked Cards

The game opened slowly. The first, second, and third hands were won by Jerry Smith. He tucked away his chips with a smile of satisfaction, as if the three hands were significant of the whole progress of the game. But Ronicky Doone pocketed his losses without either smile or sneer. He had played too often in games in the West which ran to huge prices. Miners had come in with their belts loaded with dust, eager to bet the entire sum of their winnings at once. Ranchers, fat with the profits of a good sale of cattle, had wagered the whole amount of it in a single evening. As far as large losses and large gains were concerned, Ronicky Doone was ready to handle the bets of anyone, other than millionaires, without a smile or a wince.

The trouble with McKeever was that he was playing the game too closely. Long before, it had been a maxim with the chief that a good gambler should only lose by a small margin. That maxim McKeever, playing for the first time for what he felt were important stakes in the eyes of Fernand, followed too closely. Stacking the cards, with the adeptness which years of practice had given to him, he never raised the amount of his opponent's hand beyond its own order. A pair was beaten by a pair, three of a kind was simply beaten by three of a kind of a higher order; and, when a full house was permitted by his expert dealing to appear to excite the other gamblers, he himself indulged in no more than a superior grade of three of a kind.

Half a dozen times these coincidences happened without calling for any distrust on the part of Ronicky Doone, but eventually he began to think. Steady training enabled his eyes to do what the eyes of the ordinary man could not achieve, and, while to Jerry Smith all that happened in the deals of McKeever was the height of correctness, Ronicky Doone, at the seventh deal, awakened to the fact that something was wrong.

He hardly dared to allow himself to think of anything for a time, but waited and watched, hoping against hope that Jerry Smith himself would discover the fraud which was being perpetrated on them. But Jerry Smith maintained a bland interest in the game. He had won between two and three hundred, and these winnings had been allowed by McKeever to accumulate in little runs, here and there. For nothing encourages a gambler toward reckless betting so much as a few series of high hands. He then begins to believe that he can tell, by some mysterious feeling inside, that one good hand presages another. Jerry Smith had not been brought to the point where he was willing to plunge, but he was very close to it.

McKeever was gathering the youngster in the hollow of his hand, and Ronicky Doone, fully awake and aware of all that was happening, felt a gathering rage accumulate in him. There was something doubly horrible in this cheating in this place. Ronicky set his teeth and watched. Plainly he was the chosen victim. The winnings of Jerry Smith were carefully balanced against the losses of Ronicky Doone. Hatred for this smooth-faced McKeever was waxing in him, and hatred in Ronicky Doone meant battle.

An interruption came to him from the side. It came in the form of a brief rustling of silk, like the stir of wind, and then Ruth Tolliver's coppery hair and green-blue eyes were before him—Ruth Tolliver in an evening gown and wonderful to look at. Ronicky Doone indulged himself with staring eyes, as he rose to greet her. This, then, was her chosen work under the régime of John Mark. It was as a gambler that she was great. The uneasy fire was in her eyes, the same fire that he had seen in Western gold camps, in Western gaming houses. And the delicate, nervous fingers now took on a new meaning to him.

That she had won heavily this evening he saw at once. The dangerous and impalpable flush of the gamester was on her face, and behind it burned a glow and radiance. She looked as if, having defeated men by the coolness of her wits and the favor of luck, she had begun to think that she could now outguess the world. Two men trailed behind her, stirring uneasily about when she paused at Ronicky's alcove table.

"You've found the place so soon?" she asked. "How is your luck?"

"Not nearly as good tonight as yours."

"Oh, I can't help winning. Every card I touch turns into gold this evening. I think I have the formula for it."

"Tell me, then," said Ronicky quickly enough, for there was just the shadow of a backward nod of her head.

"Just step aside. I'll spoil Mr. McKeever's game for him, I'm afraid."

Ronicky excused himself with a nod to the other two and followed the girl into the next room.

"I have bad news," she whispered instantly, "but keep smiling. Laugh if you can. The two men with me I don't know. They may be his spies for all we can tell. Ronicky Doone, John Mark is out for you. Why, in Heaven's name, are you interfering with Caroline Smith and her affairs? It will be your death, I promise you. John Mark has arrived and has placed men around the house. Ronicky Doone, he means business. Help yourself if you can. I'm unable to lift a hand for you. If I were you I should leave, and I should leave at once. Laugh, Ronicky Doone!"

He obeyed, laughing until the tears were glittering in his eyes, until the girl laughed with him.

"Good!" she whispered. "Good-by, Ronicky, and good luck."

He watched her going, saw the smiles of the two men, as they greeted her again and closed in beside her, and watched the light flash on her shoulders, as she shrugged away some shadow from her mind—perhaps the small care she had given about him. But no matter how cold-hearted she might be, how thoroughly in tune with this hard, bright world of New York, she at least was generous and had courage. Who could tell how much she risked by giving him that warning?

Ronicky went back to his place at the table, still laughing in apparent enjoyment of the jest he had just heard. He saw McKeever's ferretlike glance of interrogation and distrust—a thief's distrust of an honest man—but Ronicky's good nature did not falter in outward seeming for an instant. He swept up his hand, bet a hundred, with apparently foolish recklessness, on three sevens, and then had to buy fresh chips from McKeever.

The coming of the girl seemed to have completely upset his equilibrium as a gambler—certainly it made him bet with the recklessness of a madman. And Frederic Fernand, glancing in from time to time, watched the demolition of Ronicky's pile of chips, with growing complacence.

Ronicky Doone had allowed himself to take heed of the room about him, and Frederic Fernand liked him for it. His beautiful rooms were pearls cast before swine, so far as most of his visitors were concerned. A moment later Ronicky had risen, went toward the wall and drew a dagger from its sheath.

It was a full twelve inches in length, that blade, and it came to a point drawn out thinner than the eye could follow. The end was merely a long glint of light. As for Ronicky Doone, he cried out in surprise and then sat down, balancing the weapon in his hand and looking down at it, with the silent happiness of a child with a satisfying toy.

Frederic Fernand was observing him. There was something remarkably likable in young Doone, he decided. No matter what John Mark had said—no matter if John Mark was a genius in reading the characters of men—every genius could make mistakes. This, no doubt, was one of John Mark's mistakes. There was the free and careless thoughtlessness of a boy about this young fellow. And, though he glanced down the glimmering blade of the weapon, with a sort of sinister joy, Frederic Fernand did not greatly

care. There was more to admire in the work-
manship of the hilt than in a thousand such
blades, but a Westerner would have his eye on
the useful part of a thing.

"How much d'you think that's worth?" asked
McKeever.

"Dunno," said Ronicky. "That's good steel."

He tried the point, then he snapped it under
his thumb nail and a little shiver of a ringing
sound reached as far as Frederic Fernand.

Then he saw Ronicky Doone suddenly lean a
little across the table, pointing toward the hand
in which McKeever held the pack, ready for the
deal.

McKeever shook his head and gripped the pack
more closely.

"Do you suspect me of crooked work?" asked
McKeever. He pushed back his chair. Fernand,
studying his lieutenant in this crisis, approved of
him thoroughly. He himself was in a quandary.
Westerners fight, and a fight would be most
embarrassing. "Do you think—" began Mc-
Keever.

"I think you'll keep that hand and that same
pack of cards on the table till I've had it looked
over," said Ronicky Doone. "I've dropped a cold
thousand to you, and you're winning it with
stacked decks, McKeever."

There was a stifled oath from McKeever, as
he jerked his hand back. Frederic Fernand was
beginning to draw one breath of joy at the
thought that McKeever would escape without
having that pack, of all packs, examined, when

the long dagger flashed in the hand of Ronicky Doone.

He struck as a cat strikes when it hooks the fish out of the stream—he struck as the snapper on the end of a whiplash doubles back. And well and truly did that steel uphold its fame.

The dull, chopping sound of the blow stood by itself for an instant. Then McKeever, looking down in horror at his hand, screamed and fell back in his chair.

That was the instant when Frederic Fernand judged his lieutenant and found him wanting. A man who fainted in such a crisis as this was beyond the pale.

Other people crowded past him. Frightened, desperate, he pushed on. At length his weight enabled him to squeeze through the rapidly gathering crowd of gamblers.

The only nonchalant man of the lot was he who had actually used the weapon. For Ronicky Doone stood with his shoulders propped against the wall, his hands clasped lightly behind him. For all that, it was plain that he was not unarmed. A certain calm insolence about his expression told Frederic Fernand that the teeth of the dragon were not drawn.

"Gents," he was saying, in his mild voice, while his eyes ran restlessly from face to face, "I sure do hate to bust up a nice little party like this one has been, but I figure them cards are stacked. I got a pile of reasons for knowing, and I want somebody to look over them cards—somebody that knows stacked cards when he sees 'em. Mostly it ain't hard to get onto the order of them being run up. I'll leave it, gents, to the man that runs this dump."

And, leaning across the table, he pushed the pack straight to Frederic Fernand. The latter set his teeth. It was very cunningly done to trap him. If he said the cards were straight they might be examined afterward; and, if he were discovered in a lie, it would mean more than the loss of McKeever—it would mean the ruin of everything. Did he dare take the chance? Must he give up McKeever? The work of years of careful education had been squandered on McKeever.

Fernand looked up, and his eyes rested on the calm face of Ronicky Doone. Why had he never met a man like that before? There was an assistant! There was a fellow with steel-cold nerve—worth a thousand trained McKeevers! Then he glanced at the wounded man, cowering and bunched in his chair. At that moment the gambler made up his mind to play the game in the big way and pocket his losses.

"Ladies and gentlemen," he said sadly, placing the cards back on the edge of the table, "I am sorry to say that Mr. Doone is right. The pack has been run up. There it is for any of you to examine it. I don't pretend to understand. Most of you know that McKeever has been with me for years. Needless to say, he will be with me no more." And, turning on his heel, the old fellow walked slowly away, his hands clasped behind him, his head bowed.

And the crowd poured after him to shake his hand and tell him of their unshakable confidence in his honesty. McKeever was ruined, but the house of Frederic Fernand was more firmly established than ever, after the trial of the night.

Chapter Twenty

Trapped!

"Get the money," said Ronicky to Jerry Smith.

"There it is!"

He pointed to the drawer, where McKeever, as banker, had kept the money. The wounded man in the meantime had disappeared.

"How much is ours?" asked Jerry Smith.

"All you find there," answered Ronicky calmly.

"But there's a big bunch—large bills, too. McKeever was loaded for bear."

"He loses—the house loses it. Out in my country, Jerry, that wouldn't be half of what the house would lose for a little trick like what's been played on us tonight. Not the half of what the house would lose, I tell you! He had us trimmed, Jerry, and out West we'd wreck this joint from head to heels."

The diffident Jerry fingered the money in the drawer of the table uncertainly. Ronicky Doone swept it up and thrust it into his pocket. "We'll split straws later," said Ronicky. "Main thing we need right about now is action. This coin will start us."

In the hall, as they took their hats, they found big Frederic Fernand in the act of dissuading several of his clients from leaving. The incident of the evening was regrettable, most regrettable, but such things would happen when wild men appeared. Besides, the fault had been that of McKeever. He assured them that McKeever would never again be employed in his house. And Fernand meant it. He had discarded all care for the wounded man.

Ronicky Doone stepped to him and drew him aside. "Mr. Fernand," he said, "I've got to have a couple of words with you."

"Come into my private room," said Fernand, eager to get the fighter out of view of the rest of the little crowd. He drew Ronicky and Jerry Smith into a little apartment which opened off the hall. It was furnished with an almost feminine delicacy of style, with wide-seated, spindle-legged Louis XV. chairs and a couch covered with rich brocade. The desk was a work of Boulle. A small tapestry of the Gobelins made a ragged glow of color on the wall. Frederic Fernand had recreated an atmosphere two hundred years old.

He seated them at once. "And now, sir," he

said sternly to Ronicky Doone, "you are aware that I could have placed you in the hands of the police for what you've done tonight?"

Ronicky Doone made no answer. His only retort was a gradually spreading smile. "Partner," he said at length, while Fernand was flushing with anger at this nonchalance on the part of the Westerner, "they might of grabbed me, but they would have grabbed your house first."

"That fact," said Fernand hotly, "is the reason you have dared to act like a wild man in my place? Mr. Doone, this is your last visit."

"It sure is," said Ronicky heartily. "D'you know what would have happened out in my neck of the woods, if there had been a game like the one tonight? I wouldn't have waited to be polite, but just pulled a gat and started smashing things for luck."

"The incident is closed," Fernand said with gravity, and he leaned forward, as if to rise.

"Not by a long sight," said Ronicky Doone. "I got an idea, partner, that you worked the whole deal. This is a square house, Fernand. Why was I picked out for the dirty work?"

It required all of Fernand's long habits of self control to keep him from gasping. He managed to look Ronicky Doone fairly in the eyes. What did the youngster know? What had he guessed?

"Suppose I get down to cases and name names? The gent that talked to you about me was John Mark. Am I right?" asked Ronicky.

"Sir," said Fernand, thinking that the world was tumbling about his ears, "what infernal—"

"I'm right," said Ronicky. "I can tell when I've hurt a gent by the way his face wrinkles up. I sure hurt you that time, Fernand. John Mark it was, eh?"

Fernand could merely stare. He began to have vague fears that this young devil might have hypnotic powers, or be in touch with he knew not what unearthly source of information.

"Out with it," said Ronicky, leaving his chair.

Frederic Fernand bit his lip in thought. He was by no means a coward, and two alternatives presented themselves to him. One was to say nothing and pretend absolute ignorance; the other was to drop his hand into his coat pocket and fire the little automatic which nestled there.

"Listen," said Ronicky Doone, "suppose I was to go a little farther still in my guesses! Suppose I said I figured out that John Mark and his men might be scattered around outside this house, waiting for me and Smith to come out: What would you say to that?"

"Nothing," said Fernand, but he blinked as he spoke. "For a feat of imagination as great as that I have only a silent admiration. But, if you have some insane idea that John Mark, a gentleman I know and respect greatly, is lurking like an assassin outside the doors of my house—"

"Or maybe inside 'em," said Ronicky, unabashed by this gravity.

"If you think that," went on the gambler heavily, "I can only keep silence. But, to ease your own mind, I'll show you a simple way out of the house—a perfectly safe way which even you cannot doubt will lead you out unharmed. Does that bring you what you want?"

"It sure does," said Ronicky. "Lead the way, captain, and you'll find us right at your heels." He fell in beside Jerry Smith, while the fat man led on as their guide.

"What does he mean by a safe exit?" asked Jerry Smith. "You'd think we were in a smuggler's cave."

"Worse," said Ronicky, "a pile worse, son. And they'll sure have to have some tunnels or something for get-aways. This ain't a lawful house, Jerry."

As they talked, they were being led down toward the cellar. They paused at last in a cool, big room, paved with cement, and the unmistakable scent of the underground was in the air.

"Here we are," said the fat man, and, so saying, he turned a switch which illumined the room completely and then drew aside a curtain which opened into a black cavity.

Ronicky Doone approached and peered into it. "How does it look to you, Jerry?" he asked.

"Dark, but good enough for me, if you're all set on leaving by some funny way."

"I don't care how it looks," said Ronicky thoughtfully. "By the looks you can't make out nothing most of the time—nothing important. But they's ways of smelling things, and the smell of this here tunnel ain't too good to me. Look again and try to pry down that tunnel with your flash light, Jerry."

Accordingly Jerry raised his little pocket electric torch and held it above his head. They saw a tunnel opening, with raw dirt walls and floor and a rude framing of heavy timbers to support the roof. But it turned an angle and went out of view in a very few paces.

"Go down there with your lantern and look for the exit," said Ronicky Doone. "I'll stay back here and see that we get our farewell all fixed up."

The damp cellar air seemed to affect the throat of the fat man. He coughed heavily.

"Say, Ronicky," said Jerry Smith, "looks to me that you're carrying this pretty far. Let's take a chance on what we've got ahead of us?"

The fat man was chuckling: "You show a touching trust in me, Mr. Doone."

Ronicky turned on him with an ugly sneer. "I don't like you, Fernand," he said. "They's nothing about you that looks good to me. If I knew half as much as I guess about you I'd blow your head off, and go on without ever thinking about you again. But I don't know. Here you've got me up against it. We're going to go down that tunnel; but, if it's blind, Fernand, and you trap us from this end, it will be the worst day of your life."

"Take this passage, Doone, or turn around and come back with me, and I'll show some other ways of getting out—ways that lie under the open sky, Doone. Would you like that better? Do you want starlight and John Mark—or a little stretch of darkness, all by yourself?" asked Fernand.

Ronicky Doone studied the face of Fernand, almost wistfully. The more he knew about the fellow the more thoroughly convinced he was that Fernand was bad in all possible ways. He might be telling the truth now, however—again he might be simply tempting him on to a danger. There was only one way to decide. Ronicky, a gambler himself, mentally flipped a coin and nodded to Jerry.

"We'll go in," he said, "but man, man, how my old scars are pricking!"

They walked into the moldy, damp air of the tunnel, reached the corner, and there the passage turned and ended in a blank wall of raw dirt, with a little apron of fallen débris at the bottom of it. Ronicky Doone walked first, and, when he saw the passage obstructed in this manner, he whirled like a flash and fired at the mouth of the tunnel.

A snarl and a curse told him that he had at least come close to his target, but he was too late. A great door was sliding rapidly across the width of the tunnel, and, before he could fire a second time, the tunnel was closed.

Jerry Smith went temporarily mad. He ran at the door, which had just closed, and struck the whole weight of his body against it. There was not so much as a quiver. The face of it was smooth steel, and there was probably a dense thickness of stonework on the other side, to match the cellar walls of the house.

"It was my fool fault," exclaimed Jerry, turning to his friend. "My fault, Ronicky! Oh, what a fool I am!"

"I should have known by the feel of the scars," said Ronicky. "Put out that flash light, Jerry. We may need that after a while, and the batteries won't last forever."

He sat down, as he spoke, cross-legged, and the last thing Jerry saw, as he snapped out the light, was the lean, intense face and the blazing eyes of Ronicky Doone. Decidedly this was not a fellow to trifle with. If he trembled for himself and Ronicky, he could also spare a shudder for what would happen to Frederic Fernand, if Ronicky got away. In the meantime the light was out, and the darkness sat heavily beside and about them, with that faint succession of inaudible breathing sounds which are sensed rather than actually heard.

"Is there anything that we can do?" asked Jerry suddenly. "It's all right to sit down and argue and worry, but isn't it foolish, Ronicky?"

"How come?"

"I mean it in this way. Sometimes when you can't solve a problem it's very easy to prove that it can't be solved by anyone. That's what I can prove now, but why waste time?"

"Have we got anything special to do with our time?" asked Ronicky dryly.

"Well, my proof is easy. Here we are in hard-pan dirt, without any sort of a tool for digging. So we sure can't tunnel out from the sides, can we?"

"Looks most like we can't," said Ronicky sadly.

"And the only ways that are left are the ends."

"That's right."

"But one end is the unfinished part of the tunnel; and, if you think we can do anything to the steel door—"

"Hush up," said Ronicky. "Besides, there ain't any use in you talking in a whisper, either. No, it sure don't look like we could do much to that door. Besides, even if we could, I don't think I'd go. I'd rather take a chance against starvation than another trip to fat Fernand's place. If I ever enter it again, son, you lay to it that he'll get me bumped off, mighty pronto."

Jerry Smith, after a groan, returned to his argument. "But that ties us up, Ronicky. The door won't work, and it's worse than solid rock. And we can't tunnel out the side, without so much as a pin to help us dig, can we? I think that just about settles things. Ronicky, we can't get out."

"Suppose we had some dynamite," said Ronicky cheerily.

"Sure, but we haven't."

"Suppose we find some?"

Jerry Smith groaned. "Are you trying to make a joke out of this? Besides, could we send off a blast of dynamite in a closed tunnel like this?"

"We could try," said Ronicky. "Way I'm figuring is to show you it's bad medicine to sit down and figure out how you're beat. Even if you owe a pile of money they's some satisfaction in sitting back and adding up the figures so that you come out about a million dollars on top—in your dreams. Before we can get out of here we got to begin to feel powerful sure."

"But you take it straight, friend: Fernand ain't going to leave us in here. Nope, he's going to find a way to get us out. That's easy to figure out. But the way he'll get us out will be as dead ones, and then he can dump us, when he feels like it, in the river. Ain't that the simplest way of working it out?"

The teeth of Jerry Smith came together with a snap. "Then the thing for us to do is to get set and wait for them to make an attack?"

"No use waiting. When they attack it'll be in a way that'll give us no chance."

"Then you figure the same as me—we're lost?"

"Unless we can get out before they make the attack. In other words, Jerry, there may be something behind the dirt wall at the end of the tunnel."

"Nonsense, Ronicky."

"There's got to be," said Ronicky very soberly, "because, if there ain't, you and me are dead ones, Jerry. Come along and help me look, anyway."

Jerry rose obediently and flashed on his precious pocket torch, and they went down to pass the turn and come again to the ragged wall of earth which terminated the passage. Jerry held the torch and passed it close to the dirt. All was solid. There was no sign of anything wrong. The very pick marks were clearly defined.

"Hold on," whispered Ronicky Doone. "Hold on, Jerry. I seen something." He snatched the electric torch, and together they peered at the patch from which the dried earth had fallen.

"Queer for hardpan to break up like that," muttered Ronicky, cutting into the surface beneath the patch, with the point of his hunting knife. Instantly there was the sharp gritting of steel against steel.

The shout of Ronicky was an indrawn breath. The shout of Jerry Smith was a moan of relief.

Ronicky continued his observations. The thing was very clear. They had dug the tunnel to this point and excavated a place which they had guarded with a steel door, but, in order to conceal the hiding place, or whatever it might be, they cunningly worked the false wall of dirt against the face of it, using clay and a thin coating of plaster as a base.

"It's a place they don't use very often, maybe," said Ronicky, "and that's why they can afford to put up this fake wall of plaster and mud after every time they want to come down here. Pretty clever to leave that little pile of dirt on the floor, just like it had been worked off by the picks, eh? But we've found 'em, Jerry, and now all we got to do is to get to the door and into whatever lies beyond."

"We'd better hurry, then," cried Jerry.

"How come?"

"Take a breath."

Ronicky obeyed; the air was beginning to fill with the pungent and unmistakable odor of burning wood!

Chapter Twenty-one

The Miracle

No great intelligence was needed to understand the meaning of it. Fernand, having trapped his game, was now about to kill it. He could suffocate the two with smoke, blown into the tunnel, and make them rush blindly out. The moment they appeared, dazed and uncertain, the revolvers of half a dozen gunmen would be emptied into them.

"It's like taking a trap full of rats," said Ronicky bitterly, "and shaking them into a pail of water. Let's go back and see what we can."

They had only to turn the corner of the tunnel to be sure. Fernand had had the door of the tunnel slid noiselessly open, then, into the tunnel itself, smoking, slowly burning, pungent pieces

of pine wood had been thrown, having been first
soaked in oil, perhaps. The tunnel was rapidly
filling with smoke, and through the white drifts
of it they looked into the lighted cellar beyond.
They would run out at last, gasping for breath
and blinded by the smoke, to be shot down in a
perfect light. So much was clear.

"Now back to the wall and try to find that
door," said Ronicky.

Jerry had already turned. In a moment they
were back and tearing with their fingers at the
sham wall, kicking loose fragments with their
feet.

All the time, while they cleared a larger and
larger space, they searched feverishly with the
electric torch for some sign of a knob which
would indicate a door, or some button or spring
which might be used to open it. But there was
nothing, and in the meantime the smoke was
drifting back, in more and more unendurable
clouds.

"I can't stand much more," declared Jerry at
length.

"Keep low. The best air is there," answered
Ronicky.

A voice called from the mouth of the tunnel,
and they could recognize the smooth tongue of
Frederic Fernand. "Doone, I think I have you
now. But trust yourselves to me, and all may
still be well with you. Throw out your weapons,
and then walk out yourselves, with your arms
above your heads, and you may have a second
chance. I don't promise—I simply offer you a

hope in the place of no hope at all. Is that a good bargain?"

"I'll see you hung first," answered Ronicky and turned again to his work at the wall.

But it seemed a quite hopeless task. The surface of the steel was still covered, after they had cleared it as much as they could, with a thin, clinging coat of plaster which might well conceal the button or device for opening the door. Every moment the task became infinitely harder.

Finally Jerry, his lungs nearly empty of oxygen, cast himself down on the floor and gasped. A horrible gagging sound betrayed his efforts for breath.

Ronicky knelt beside him. His own lungs were burning, and his head was thick and dizzy. "One more try, then we'll turn and rush them and die fighting, Jerry."

The other nodded and started to his feet. Together they made that last effort, fumbling with their hands across the rough surface, and suddenly—had they touched the spring, indeed?—a section of the surface before them swayed slowly in. Ronicky caught the half-senseless body of Jerry Smith and thrust him inside. He himself staggered after, and before him stood Ruth Tolliver!

While he lay panting on the floor, she closed the door through which they had come and then stood and silently watched them. Presently Smith sat up, and Ronicky Doone staggered to his feet, his head clearing rapidly.

He found himself in a small room, not more than eight feet square, with a ceiling so low that he could barely stand erect. As for the furnishings and the arrangement, it was more like the inside of a safe than anything else. There were, to be sure, three little stools, but nothing else that one would expect to find in an apartment. For the rest there was nothing but a series of steel drawers and strong chests, lining the walls of the room and leaving in the center very little room in which one might move about.

He had only a moment to see all of this. Ruth Tolliver, hooded in an evening cloak, but with the light gleaming in her coppery hair, was shaking him by the arm and leaning a white face close to him.

"Hurry!" she was saying. "There isn't a minute to lose. You must start now, at once. They will find out—they will guess—and then—"

"John Mark?" he asked.

"Yes," she exclaimed, realizing that she had said too much, and she pressed her hand over her mouth, looking at Ronicky Doone in a sort of horror.

Jerry Smith had come to his feet at last, but he remained in the background, staring with a befuddled mind at the lovely vision of the girl. Fear and excitement and pleasure had transformed her face, but she seemed trembling in an agony of desire to be gone. She seemed invincibly drawn to remain there longer still. Ronicky Doone stared at her, with a strange blending of pity and admiration. He knew that the danger was not over by any means, but he began to forget that.

"This way!" called the girl and led toward an opposite door, very low in the wall.

"Lady," said Ronicky gently, "will you hold on one minute? They won't start to go through the smoke for a while. They'll think they've choked us, when we don't come out on the rush, shooting. But they'll wait quite a time to make sure. They don't like my style so well that they'll hurry me." He smiled sourly at the thought. "And we got time to learn a lot of things that we'll never find out, unless we know right now, pronto!"

He stepped before the girl, as he spoke. "How come you knew we were in there? How come you to get down here? How come you to risk everything you got to let us out through the treasure room of Mark's gang?"

He had guessed as shrewdly as he could, and he saw, by her immediate wincing, that the shot had told.

"You strange, mad, wild Westerner!" she exclaimed. "Do you mean to tell me you want to stay here and talk? Even if you have a moment to spare you must use it. If you knew the men with whom you are dealing you would never dream of—"

In her pause he said, smiling: "Lady, it's tolerable clear that you don't know me. But the way I figure it is this: a gent may die any time, but, when he finds a minute for good living, he'd better make the most of it."

He knew by her eyes that she half guessed his

meaning, but she wished to be certain. "What do you intend by that?" she asked.

"It's tolerable simple," said Ronicky. "I've seen square things done in my life, but I've never yet seen a girl throw up all she had to do a good turn for a gent she's seen only once. You follow me, lady? I pretty near guess the trouble you're running into."

"You guess what?" she asked.

"I guess that you're one of John Mark's best cards. You're his chief gambler, lady, and he uses you on the big game."

She had drawn back, one hand pressed against her breast, her mouth tight with the pain. "You have guessed all that about me?" she asked faintly. "That means you despise me!"

"What folks do don't matter so much," said Ronicky. "It's the reasons they have for doing a thing that matters, I figure, and the way they do it. I dunno how John Mark hypnotized you and made a tool out of you, but I do know that you ain't changed by what you've done."

Ronicky Doone stepped to her quickly and took both her hands. He was not, ordinarily, particularly forward with girls. Now he acted as gracefully as if he had been the father of Ruth Tolliver. "Lady," he said, "you've saved two lives tonight. That's a tolerable lot to have piled up to anybody's credit. Besides, inside you're snow-white. We've got to go, but I'm coming back. Will you let me come back?"

"Never, never!" declared Ruth Tolliver. "You must never see me—you must never see Caroline

Smith again. Any step you take in that direction is under peril of your life. Leave New York, Ronicky Doone. Leave it as quickly as you may, and never come back. Only pray that his arm isn't long enough to follow you."

"Leave Caroline?" he asked. "I'll tell you what you're going to do, Ruth. When you get back home you're going to tell Caroline that Jerry, here, has seen the light about Mark, and that he has money enough to pay back what he owes."

"But I haven't," broke in Jerry.

"I have it," said Ronicky, "and that's the same thing."

"I'll take no charity," declared Jerry Smith.

"You'll do what I tell you," said Ronicky Doone. "You been bothering enough, son. Go tell Caroline what I've said," he went on to the girl. "Let her know that they's no chain on anybody, and, if she wants to find Bill Gregg, all she's got to do is go across the street. You understand?"

"But, even if I were to tell her, how could she go, Ronicky Doone, when she's watched?"

"If she can't make a start and get to a man that loves her and is waiting for her, right across the street, she ain't worth worrying about," said Ronicky sternly. "Do we go this way?"

She hurried before them. "You've waited too long—you've waited too long!" she kept whispering in her terror, as she led them through the door, paused to turn out the light behind her, and then conducted them down a passage like that on the other side of the treasure chamber.

It was all deadly black and deadly silent, but the rustling of the girl's dress, as she hurried before them, was their guide. And always her whisper came back: "Hurry! Hurry! I fear it is too late!"

Suddenly they were climbing up a narrow flight of steps. They stood under the starlight in a back yard, with houses about them on all sides.

"Go down that alley, and you will be on the street," said the girl. "Down that alley, and then hurry—run—find the first taxi. Will you do that?"

"We'll sure go, and we'll wait for Caroline Smith—and you, too!"

"Don't talk madness! Why will you stay? You risk everything for yourselves and for me!"

Jerry Smith was already tugging at Ronicky's arm to draw him away, but the Westerner was stubbornly pressing back to the girl. He had her hand and would not leave it.

"If you don't show up, lady," he said, "I'll come to find you. You hear?"

"No, no!"

"I swear!"

"Bless you, but never venture near again. But, oh, Ronicky Doone, I wish ten other men in the whole world could be half so generous and wild as you!" Suddenly her hand was slipped from his, and she was gone into the shadows.

Down the alley went Jerry Smith, but he returned in an agony of dread to find that Ronicky Doone was still running here and there, in a blind confusion, probing the shadowy corners of the yard in search of the girl.

"Come off, you wild man," said Jerry. "They'll be on our heels any minute—they may be waiting for us now, down the alley—come off, idiot, quick!"

"If I thought they was a chance of finding her I'd stay," declared Ronicky, shaking his head bitterly. "Whether you and me live, don't count beside a girl like that. Getting soot on one tip of her finger might mean more'n whether you or me die."

"Maybe, maybe," said the other, "but answer that tomorrow; right now, let's start to make sure of ourselves, and we can come back to find her later."

Ronicky Doone, submitting partly to the force and partly to the persuasion of his friend, turned reluctantly and followed him down the alley.

Chapter Twenty-two

Mark Makes a Move

Passing hurriedly out of the cloakroom, a little later, Ruth met Simonds, the lieutenant of Frederic Fernand, in the passage. He was a ratfaced little man, with a furtive smile. Not an unpleasant smile, but it was continually coming and going, as if he wished earnestly to win the favor of the men before him, but greatly doubted his ability to do so. Ruth Tolliver, knowing his genius for the cards, knowing his cold and unscrupulous soul, detested him heartily.

When she saw his eyes flicker up and down the hall she hesitated. Obviously he wished to speak with her, and obviously he did not wish to be seen in the act. As she paused he stepped to her, his face suddenly set with determination.

"Watch John Mark," he whispered. "Don't trust him. He suspects everything!"

"What? Everything about what?" she asked.

Simonds gazed at her for a moment with a singular expression. There were conjoined cynicism, admiration, doubt, and fear in his glance. But, instead of speaking again, he bowed and slipped away into the open hall.

She heard him call, and she heard Fernand's oily voice make answer. And at that she shivered.

What had Simonds guessed? How, under heaven, did he know where she had gone when she left the gaming house? Or did he know? Had he not merely guessed? Perhaps he had been set on by Fernand or Mark to entangle and confuse her?

There remained, out of all this confusion of guesswork, a grim feeling that Simonds did indeed know, and that, for the first time in his life, perhaps, he was doing an unbought, a purely generous thing.

She remembered, now, how often Simonds had followed her with his eyes, how often his face had lighted when she spoke even casually to him. Yes, there might be a reason for Simonds' generosity. But that implied that he knew fairly well what John Mark himself half guessed. The thought that she was under the suspicion of Mark himself was terrible to her.

She drew a long breath and advanced courageously into the gaming rooms.

The first thing she saw was Fernand hurrying a late comer toward the tables, laughing and chatting as he went. She shuddered at the sight of him. It was strange that he, who had, a moment before, in the very cellar of that house, been working to bring about the death of two men, should now be immaculate, self-possessed.

A step farther and she saw John Mark sitting at a console table, with his back to the room and a cup of tea before him. That was, in fact, his favorite drink at all hours of the day or night. To see Fernand was bad enough, but to see the master mind of all the evil that passed around her was too much. The girl inwardly thanked Heaven that his back was turned and started to pass him as softly as possible.

"Just a minute, Ruth," he called, as she was almost at the door of the room.

For a moment there was a frantic impulse in her to bolt like a foolish child afraid of the dark. In the next apartment were light and warmth and eager faces and smiles and laughter, and here, behind her, was the very spirit of darkness calling her back. After an imperceptible hesitation she turned.

Mark had not turned in his chair, but it was easy to discover how he had known of her passing. A small oval mirror, fixed against the wall before him, had shown her image. How much had it betrayed, she wondered, of her guiltily stealthy pace? She went to him and found that he was leisurely and openly examining her in the glass, as she approached, his chin resting on one hand, his thin face perfectly calm, his eyes hazy with content. It was a habit of his to regard her like a picture, but she had never become used to it; she was always disconcerted by it, as she was at this moment.

He rose, of course, when she was beside him, and asked her to sit down.

"But I've hardly touched a card," she said. "This isn't very professional, you know, wasting a whole evening."

She was astonished to see him flush to the roots of his hair. His voice shook. "Sit down, please."

She obeyed, positively inert with surprise.

"Do you think I keep you at this detestable business because I want the money?" he asked. "Dear Heaven! Ruth, is that what you think of me?" Fortunately, before she could answer, he went on: "No, no, no! I have wanted to make you a free and independent being, my dear, and that is why I have put you through the most dangerous and exacting school in the world. You understand?"

"I think I do," she replied falteringly.

"But not entirely. Let me pour you some tea? No?"

He sighed, as he blew forth the smoke of a cigarette. "But you don't understand entirely," he continued, "and you must. Go back to the old days, when you knew nothing of the world but me. Can you remember?"

"Yes, yes!"

"Then you certainly recall a time when, if I had simply given directions, you would have been mine, Ruth. I could have married you the moment you became a woman. Is that true?"

"Yes," she whispered, "that is perfectly true."

The coldness that passed over her taught her for the first time how truly she dreaded that marriage which had been postponed, but which inevitably hung over her head.

"But I didn't want such a wife," continued John Mark. "You would have been an undeveloped child, really; you would never have grown up. No matter what they say, something about a woman is cut off at the root when she marries. Certainly, if she had not been free before, she is a slave if she marries a man with a strong will. And I have a strong will, Ruth—very strong!"

"Very strong, John," she whispered again.

He smiled faintly, as if there were less of what he wanted in that second use of the name. He went on: "So you see, I faced a problem. I must and would marry you. There was never any other woman born who was meant for me. So much so good. But, if I married you before you were wise enough to know me, you would have become a slave, shrinking from me, yielding to me, incapable of loving me. No, I wanted a free and independent creature as my wife; I wanted a partnership, you see. Put you into the world, then, and let you see men and women? No, I could not do that in the ordinary way. I have had to show you the hard and bad side of life, because I am, in many ways, a hard and bad man myself!"

He said it, almost literally, through his teeth. His face was fierce, defying her—his eyes were wistful, entreating her not to agree with him. Such a sudden rush of pity for the man swept over her that she put out her hand and pressed his. He looked down at her hand for a moment, and she felt his fingers trembling under that gentle pressure.

"I understand more now," she said slowly, "than I have ever understood before. But I'll never understand entirely."

"A thing that's understood entirely is despised," he said, with a careless sweep of his hand. "A thing that is understood is not feared. I wish to be feared, not to make people cower, but to make them know when I come, and when I go. Even love is nothing without a seasoning of fear. For instance"—he flushed as the torrent of his speech swept him into a committal of himself— "I am afraid of you, dear girl. Do you know what I have done with the money you've won?"

"Tell me," she said curiously, and, at the same time, she glanced in wonder, as a servant passed softly across the little room. Was it not stranger than words could tell that such a man as John Mark should be sitting in this almost public place and pouring his soul out into the ear of a girl?

"I shall tell you," said Mark, his voice softening. "I have contributed half of it to charity."

Her lips, compressed with doubt, parted in wonder. "Charity!" she exclaimed.

"And the other half," he went on, "I deposited in a bank to the credit of a fictitious personality. That fictitious personality is, in flesh and blood, Ruth Tolliver with a new name. You understand? I have only to hand you the bank book with the list of deposits, and you can step out of this Tolliver personality and appear in a new part of the world as another being. Do you see what it means? If, at the last, you find you cannot marry me, my dear, you are provided for. Not out of my charity, which would be bitter to you, but out of your own earnings. And, lest you should be horrified at the thought of living on your earnings at the gaming table, I have thrown bread on the waters, dear Ruth. For every dollar you have in the bank you have given another to charity, and both, I hope, have borne interest for you!"

His smile faded a little, as she murmured, with her glance going past him: "Then I am free? Free, John?"

"Whenever you wish!"

"Not that I ever shall wish, but to know that I am not chained, that is the wonderful thing." She looked directly at him again: "I never dreamed there was so much fineness in you, John Mark, I never dreamed it, but I should have!"

"Now I have been winning Caroline to the game," he went on, "and she is beginning to love it. In another year, or six months, trust me to have completely filled her with the fever. But now enters the mischief-maker in the piece, a stranger, an ignorant outsider. This incredible man arrives and, in a few days, having miraculously run Caroline to earth, goes on and brings

Caroline face to face with her lover, teaches Jerry Smith that I am his worst enemy, gets enough money to pay off his debt to me, and convinces him that I can never use my knowledge of his crime to jail him, because I don't dare bring the police too close to my own rather explosive record."

"I saw them both here!" said the girl. She wondered how much he guessed, and she saw his keen eyes probe her with a glance. But her ingenuousness, if it did not disarm him, at least dulled the edge of his suspicions.

"He was here, and the trap was laid here, and he slipped through it. Got away through a certain room which Fernand would give a million to keep secret. At any rate the fellow has shown that he is slippery and has a sting, too. He sent a bullet a fraction of an inch past Fernand's head, at one point in the little story.

"In short, the price is too high. What I want is to secure Caroline Smith from the inside. I want you to go to her, to persuade her to go away with you on a trip. Take her to the Bermudas, or to Havana—any place you please. The moment the Westerner thinks his lady is running away from him of her own volition he'll throw up his hands and curse his luck and go home. They have that sort of pride on the other side of the Rockies. Will you go back tonight, right now, and persuade Caroline to go with you?'

She bowed her head under the shock of it. Ronicky Doone had begged her to send Caroline

Smith to meet her lover. Now the counterattack followed.

"Do you think she'd listen?"

"Yes, tell her that the one thing that will save the head of Bill Gregg is for her to go away, otherwise I'll wipe the fool off the map. Better still, tell her that Gregg of his own free will has left New York and given up the chase. Tell her you want to console her with a trip. She'll be sad and glad and flattered, all in the same moment, and go along with you without a word. Will you try, Ruth?"

"I suppose you would have Bill Gregg removed—if he continued a nuisance?"

"Not a shadow of a doubt. Will you do your best?"

She rose. "Yes," said the girl. Then she managed to smile at him. "Of course I'll do my best. I'll go back right now."

He took her arm to the door of the room. "Thank Heaven," he said, "that I have one person in whom I can trust without question—one who needs no bribing or rewards, but works to please me. Good-by, my dear."

He watched her down the hall and then turned and went through room after room to the rear of the house. There he rapped on a door in a peculiar manner. It was opened at once, and Harry Morgan appeared before him.

"A rush job, Harry," he said. "A little shadowing."

Harry jerked his cap lower over his eyes. "Gimme the smell of the trail, I'm ready," he said.

"Ruth Tolliver has just left the house. Follow her. She'll probably go home. She'll probably talk with Caroline Smith. Find a way of listening. If you hear anything that seems wrong to you—anything about Caroline leaving the house alone, for instance, telephone to me at once. Now go and work, as you never worked for me before."

Chapter Twenty-three

Caroline takes Command

Ruth left the gaming house of Frederic Fernand
entirely convinced that she must do as John Mark
had told her—work for him as she had never
worked before. The determination made her go
home to Beekman Place as fast as a taxicab would
whirl her along.

It was not until she had climbed to Caroline
Smith's room and opened the door that her
determination faltered. For there she saw the
girl lying on her bed weeping. And it seemed
to the poor, bewildered brain of Ruth Tolliver,
as if the form of Ronicky Doone, passionate and
eager as before, stood at her side and begged
her again to send Caroline Smith across the
street to a lifelong happiness, and she could

do it. Though Mark had ordered the girl to be confined to her room until further commands were given on the subject, no one in the house would think of questioning Ruth Tolliver, if she took the girl downstairs to the street and told her to go on her way.

She closed the door softly and, going to the bed, touched the shoulder of Caroline. The poor girl sat up slowly and turned a stained and swollen face to Ruth. If there was much to be pitied there was something to be laughed at, also. Ruth could not forbear smiling. But Caroline was clutching at her hands.

"He's changed his mind?" she asked eagerly. "He's sent you to tell me that he's changed his mind, Ruth? Oh, you've persuaded him to it— like an angel—I know you have!"

Ruth Tolliver freed herself from the reaching hands, moistened the end of a towel in the bathroom and began to remove the traces of tears from the face of Caroline Smith. That face was no longer flushed, but growing pale with excitement and hope.

"It's true?" she kept asking. "It is true, Ruth?"

"Do you love him as much as that?"

"More than I can tell you—so much more!"

"Try to tell me then, dear."

Talking of her love affair began to brighten the other girl, and now she managed a wan smile. "His letters were very bad. But, between the lines, I could read so much real manhood, such simple honesty, such a heart, such a will to trust! Ruth, are you laughing at me?"

"No, no, far from that! It's a thrilling thing to hear, my dear."

For she was remembering that in another man there might be found these same qualities. Not so much simplicity, perhaps, but to make up for it, a great fire of will and driving energy.

"But I didn't actually know that I was in love. Even when I made the trip West and wrote to him to meet the train on my return—even then I was only guessing. When he didn't appear at the station I went cold and made up my mind that I would never think of him again."

"But when you saw him in the street, here?"

"John Mark had prepared me and hardened me against that meeting, and I was afraid even to think for myself. But, when Ronicky Doone— bless him!—talked to me in your room, I knew what Bill Gregg must be, since he had a friend who would venture as much for him as Ronicky Doone did. It all came over me in a flash. I did love him—I did, indeed!"

"Yes, yes," whispered Ruth Tolliver, nodding and smiling faintly. "I remember how he stood there and talked to you. He was like a man on fire. No wonder that a spark caught in you, Caroline. He—he's a—very fine-looking fellow, don't you think, Caroline?"

"Bill Gregg? Yes, indeed."

"I mean Ronicky."

"Of course! Very handsome!"

There was something in the voice of Caroline that made Ruth look down sharply to her face, but the girl was clever enough to mask her excitement and delight.

"Afterward, when you think over what he has said, it isn't a great deal, but at the moment he seems to know a great deal—about what's going on inside one, don't you think, Caroline?"

These continual appeals for advice, appeals from the infallible Ruth Tolliver, set the heart of Caroline beating. There was most certainly something in the wind.

"I think he does," agreed Caroline, masking her eyes. "He has a way, when he looks at you, of making you feel that he isn't thinking of anything else in the world but you."

"Does he have that same effect on every one?" asked Ruth. She added, after a moment of thought, "Yes, I suppose it's just a habit of his. I wish I knew."

"Why?" queried Caroline, unable to refrain from the stinging little question.

"Oh, for no good reason—just that he's an odd character. In my work, you know, one has to study character. Ronicky Doone is a different sort of man, don't you think?"

"Very different, dear."

Then a great inspiration came to Caroline. Ruth was a key which, she knew, could unlock nearly any door in the house of John Mark.

"Do you know what we are going to do?" she asked gravely, rising.

"Well?"

"We're going to open that door together, and we're going down the stairs—together."

"Together? But we—Don't you know John Mark has given orders—"

"That I'm not to leave the room. What difference does that make? They won't dare stop us if you are with me, leading the way."

"Caroline, are you mad? When I come back—"

"You're not coming back."

"Not coming back!"

"No, you're going on with me!"

She took Ruth by the arms and turned her until the light struck into her eyes. Ruth Tolliver, aghast at this sudden strength in one who had always been a meek follower, obeyed without resistance.

"But where?" she demanded.

"Where I'm going."

"What?"

"To Ronicky Doone, my dear. Don't you see?"

The insistence bewildered Ruth Tolliver. She felt herself driven irresistibly forward, with or without her own will.

"Caroline," she protested, trying feebly to free herself from the commanding hands and eyes of her companion, "are you quite mad? Go to him? Why should I? How can I?"

"Not as I'm going to Bill Gregg, with my heart in my hands, but to ask Ronicky Doone—bless him!—to take you away somewhere, so that you can begin a new life. Isn't that simple?"

"Ask charity of a stranger?"

"You know he isn't a stranger, and you know it isn't charity. He'll be happy. He's the kind that's happy when he's being of use to others?"

"Yes," answered Ruth Tolliver, "of course he is."

"And you'd trust him?"

"To the end of the world. But to leave—"

"Ruth, you've kept cobwebs before your eyes so long that you don't see what's happening around you. John Mark hypnotizes you. He makes you think that the whole world is bad, that we are simply making capital out of our crimes. As a matter of fact, the cold truth is that he has made me a thief, Ruth, and he has made you something almost as bad— a gambler!"

The follower had become the leader, and she was urging Ruth Tolliver slowly to the door. Ruth was protesting—she could not throw herself on the kindness of Ronicky Doone—it could not be done. It would be literally throwing herself at his head. But here the door opened, and she allowed herself to be led out into the hall. They had not made more than half a dozen steps down its dim length when the guard hurried toward them.

"Talk to him," whispered Caroline Smith. "He's come to stop me, and you're the only person who can make him let me pass on!"

The guard hurriedly came up to them. "Sorry," he said. "Got an idea you're going downstairs, Miss Smith."

"Yes," she said faintly.

The fellow grinned. "Not yet. You'll stay up here till the chief gives the word. And I got to ask you to step back into your room, and step

214

quick." His voice grew harsh, and he came closer. "He told me straight, you're not to come out."

Caroline had shrunk back, and she was on the verge of turning when the arm of Ruth was passed strongly around her shoulders and stayed her.

"She's going with me," she told John Mark's bulldog. "Does that make a difference to you?"

He ducked his head and grinned feebly in his anxiety. "Sure it makes a difference. You go where you want, any time you want, but this—"

"I say she's going with me, and I'm responsible for her."

She urged Caroline forward, and the latter made a step, only to find that she was directly confronted by the guard.

"I got my orders," he said desperately to Ruth.

"Do you know who I am?" she asked hotly.

"I know who you are," he answered, "and, believe me, I would not start bothering you none, but I got to keep this lady back. I got the orders."

"They're old orders," insisted Ruth Tolliver, "and they have been changed."

"Not to my knowing," replied the other, less certain in his manner.

Ruth seized the critical moment to say: "Walk on, Caroline. If he blocks your way—" She did not need to finish the sentence, for, as Caroline started on, the guard slunk sullenly to one side of the corridor.

"It ain't my doings," he said. "But they got two bosses in this joint, and one of them is a girl. How can a gent have any idea which way he ought to step in a pinch? Go on, Miss Smith, but you'll be answered for!"

They hardly heard the last of these words, as they turned down the stairway, hurrying, but not fast enough to excite the suspicion of the man behind them.

"Oh, Ruth," whispered Caroline Smith. "Oh, Ruth!"

"It was close," said Ruth Tolliver, "but we're through. And, now that I'm about to leave it, I realize how I've hated this life all these years. I'll never stop thanking you for waking me up to it, Caroline."

They reached the floor of the lower hall, and a strange thought came to Ruth. She had hurried home to execute the bidding of John Mark. She had left it, obeying the bidding of Ronicky Doone.

They scurried to the front door. As they opened it the sharp gust of night air blew in on them, and they heard the sound of a man running up the steps. In a moment the dim hall light showed on the slender form and the pale face of John Mark standing before them.

Caroline felt the start of Ruth Tolliver. For her part she was on the verge of collapse, but a strong pressure from the hand of her companion told her that she had an ally in the time of need.

216

"Tut tut!" Mark was saying, "what's this? How did Caroline get out of her room—and with you, Ruth?"

"It's idiotic to keep her locked up there all day and all night, in weather like this," said Ruth, with a perfect calm that restored Caroline's courage almost to the normal. "When I talked to her this evening I made up my mind that I'd take her out for a walk."

"Well," replied John Mark, "that might not be so bad. Let's step inside and talk it over for a moment."

They retreated, and he entered and clicked the door behind him. "The main question is, where do you intend to walk?"

"Just in the street below the house."

"Which might not lead you across to the house on the other side?"

"Certainly not! I shall be with her."

"But suppose both of you go into that house, and I lose two birds instead of one? What of that, my clever Ruth?"

She knew at once, by something in his voice rather than his words, that he had managed to learn the tenor of the talk in Caroline's room. She asked bluntly: "What are you guessing at?"

"Nothing. I only speak of what I know. No single pair of ears is enough for a busy man. I have to hire help, and I get it. Very effective help, too, don't you agree?"

"Eavesdropping!" exclaimed Ruth bitterly. "Well—it's true, John Mark. You sent me to steal her from her lover, and I've tried to steal her for him in the end. Do you know why? Because she was able to show me what a happy love might mean to a woman. She showed me that, and she showed me how much courage love had given her. So I began to guess a good many things, and, among the rest, I came to the conclusion that I could never truly love you, John Mark.

"I've spoken quickly," she went on at last. "It isn't that I have feared you all the time—I haven't been playing a part, John, on my word. Only—tonight I learned something new. Do you see?"

"Heaven be praised," said John Mark, "that we all have the power of learning new things, now and again. I congratulate you. Am I to suppose that Caroline was your teacher?"

He turned from her and faced Caroline Smith, and, though he smiled on her, there was a quality in the smile that shriveled her very soul with fear. No matter what he might say or do this evening to establish himself in the better graces of the girl he was losing, his malice was not dead. That she knew.

"She was my teacher," answered Ruth steadily, "because she showed me, John, what a marvelous thing it is to be free. You understand that all the years I have been with you I have never been free?"

"Not free?" he asked, the first touch of emotion showing in his voice. "Not free, my dear? Was there ever the least wish of yours since you were a child that I did not gratify? Not one, Ruth; not one, surely, of which I am conscious!"

"Because I had no wishes," she answered slowly, "that were not suggested by something that you liked or disliked. You were the starting point of all that I desired. I was almost afraid to think until I became sure that you approved of my thinking."

"That was long ago," he said gravely. "Since those old days I see you have changed greatly."

"Because of the education you gave me," she answered.

"Yes, yes, that was the great mistake. I begin to see. Heaven, one might say, gave you to me. I felt that I must improve on the gift of Heaven before I accepted you. There was my fault. For that I must pay the great penalty. Kismet! And now, what is it you wish?"

"To leave at once."

"A little harsh, but necessary, if you will it. There is the door, free to you. The change of identity of which I spoke to you is easily arranged. I have only to take you to the bank and that is settled. Is there anything else?"

"Only one thing—and that is not much."

"Very good."

"You have given so much," she ran on eagerly, "that you will give one thing more—out of the goodness of that really big heart of yours, John, dear!"

He winced under that pleasantly tender word.

And she said: "I want to take Caroline with me—to freedom and the man she loves. That is really all!"

The lean fingers of John Mark drummed on the back of the chair, while he smiled down on her, an inexplicable expression on his face.

"Only that?" he asked. "My dear, how strange you women really are! After all these years of study I should have thought that you would, at least, have partially comprehended me. I see that is not to be. But try to understand that I divide with a nice distinction the affairs of sentiment and the affairs of business. There is only one element in my world of sentiment—that is you. Therefore, ask what you want and take it for yourself; but for Caroline, that is an entirely different matter. No, Ruth, you may take what you will for yourself, but for her, for any other living soul, not a penny, not a cent will I give. Can you comprehend it? Is it clear? As for giving her freedom, nothing under Heaven could persuade me to it!"

Chapter Twenty-four

The Ultimate Sacrifice

She stared at him, as the blow fell, and then her glance turned slowly to Caroline who had uttered a sharp cry and sunk into a chair.

"Help me, Ruth," she implored pitifully. "No other person in the world can help me but you!"

"Do you see that," asked Ruth quietly of John Mark, "and still it doesn't move you?"

"Not a hairbreadth, my dear."

"But isn't it absurd? Suppose I have my freedom, and I tell the police that in this house a girl against her will—"

"Tush, my dear! You really do not know me at all. Do you think they can reach me? She may be a hundred miles away before you have spoken en words to the authorities."

"But I warn you that all your holds on her are broken. She knows that you have no holds over her brother. She knows that Ronicky Doone has broken them all—that Jerry is free of you!"

"Ronicky Doone," said Mark, his face turning gray, "is a talented man. No doubt of it; his is a very peculiar and incisive talent, I admit. But, though he has broken all the old holds, there are ways of finding new ones. If you leave now, I can even promise you, my dear, that, before the next day dawns, the very soul of Caroline will be a pawn in my hands. Do you doubt it? Such an exquisitely tender, such a delicate soul as Caroline, can you doubt that I can form invisible bonds which will hold her even when she is a thousand miles away from me? Tush, my dear; think again, and you will think better of my ability."

"Suppose," Ruth said, "I were to offer to stay?"

He bowed. "You tempt me, with such overwhelming generosity, to become even more generous myself and set her free at once. But, alas, I am essentially a practical man. If you will stay with me, Ruth, if you marry me at once, why, then indeed this girl is as free as the wind. Otherwise I should be a fool. You see, my dear, I love you so that I must have you by fair means or foul, but I cannot put any chain upon you except your own word. I confess it, you see, even before this poor girl, if she is capable of understanding, which I doubt. But speak again—do you make the offer?"

She hesitated, and he went on: "Be careful. I have had you once, and I have lost you, it seems. If I have you again there is no power in you— no power between earth and heaven to take you from me a second time. Give yourself to me with a word, and I shall make you mine forever. Then Caroline shall go free—free as the wind—to her lover, my dear, who is waiting."

He made no step toward her, and he kept his voice smooth and clear. Had he done otherwise he knew that she would have shrunk. She looked to him, she looked to Caroline Smith. The latter had suddenly raised her head and thrown out her hands, with an unutterable appeal in her eyes. At that mute appeal Ruth Tolliver surrendered.

"It's enough," she said. "I think there would be no place for me after all. What could I do in the world except what you've taught me to do? No, let Caroline go freely, and I give my—"

"Stop!"

He checked her with his raised hand, and his eyes blazed and glittered in the dead whiteness of his face. "Don't give me your word, my dear. I don't want that chain to bind you. There might come a time when some power arose strong enough to threaten to take you from me. Then I want to show you that I don't need your promise. I can hold you for myself. Only come to me and tell me simply that you will be mine if you can. Will you do that?"

She crossed the room slowly and stood before him. "I will do that," she said faintly, half closing her eyes. She had come so close that, if he willed, he could have taken her in his arms. She nerved herself against it; then she felt her hand taken, raised and touched lightly against trembling lips. When she stepped back she knew that the decisive moment of her life had been passed.

"You are free to go," said John Mark to Caroline. "Therefore don't wait. Go at once."

"Ruth!" whispered the girl.

Ruth Tolliver turned away, and the movement brought Caroline beside her, with a cry of pain. "Is it what I think?" she asked. "Are you making the sacrifice all for me? You don't really care for him, Ruth, and—"

"Caroline!" broke in John Mark.

She turned at the command of that familiar voice, as if she had been struck with a whip. He had raised the curtain of the front window beside the door and was pointing up and across the street.

"I see the window of Gregg's room," he said. "A light has just appeared in it. I suppose he is waiting. But, if you wish to go, your time is short—very short!"

An infinite threat was behind the calmness of the voice. She could only say to Ruth: "I'll never forget." Then she fled down the hall and through the door, and the two within heard the sharp patter of her heels, as she ran down to the street

It was freedom for Caroline, and Ruth, lifting her eyes, looked into the face of the man she was to marry. She could have held out, she felt had it not been for the sound of those departing footsteps, running so blithely toward a lifetime of happiness. Even as it was she made herself hold out. Then a vague astonishment came to clear her mind. There was no joy in the face of John Mark, only a deep and settled pain.

"You see," he said, with a smile of anguish, "I have done it. I have bought the thing I love, and that, you know, is the last and deepest damnation. If another man had told me that I was capable of such a thing, I'd have killed him on the spot. But now I have done it!"

"I think I'll go up to my room," she answered, her eyes on the floor. She made herself raise them to his. "Unless you wish to talk to me longer?"

She saw him shudder.

"If you can help it," he said, "don't make me see the brand I have put on you. Don't, for Heaven's sake, cringe to me if you can help it."

"Very well," she said.

He struck his clenched hand against his face. "It's the price," he declared through his teeth, "and I accept it." He spoke more to himself than to her, and then directly: "Will you let me walk up with you?"

"Yes."

He took her passive arm. They went slowly, slowly up the stairs, for at each landing it seemed her strength gave out, and she had to pause for a brief rest; when she paused he spoke with difficulty, but with his heart in every word.

"You remember the old Greek fable, Ruth? The story about all the pains and torments

which flew out of Pandora's box, and how
Hope came out last—that blessed Hope—and
healed the wounds? Here, a moment after the
blow has fallen, I am hoping again like a fool. I
am hoping that I shall teach you to forget; or, if I
cannot teach you to forget, than I shall even make
you glad of what you have done tonight."

The door closed on her, and she was alone.
Raising her head she found she was looking
straight across the street to the lighted windows
of the rooms of Ronicky Doone and Bill Gregg.
While she watched she saw the silhouette of a
man and woman running to each other, saw
them clasped in each other's arms. Ruth dropped
to her knees and buried her face in her hands.

Chapter Twenty-five

Unhappy Freedom

Once out in the street Caroline had cast one glance of terror over her shoulder at the towering facade of the house of John Mark, then she fled, as fast as her feet would carry her, straight across the street and up the steps of the rooming house and frantically up the stairs, a panic behind her.

Presently she was tapping hurriedly and loudly on a door, while, with her head turned, she watched for the coming of some swift-avenging figure from behind. John Mark had given her up, but it was impossible for John Mark to give up anything. When would he strike? That was the only question.

Then the door opened. The very light that

poured out into the dim hall was like the reach of a friendly hand, and there was Ronicky Doone laughing for pure joy—and there was Bill Gregg's haggard face, as if he saw a ghost.

"I told you, Bill, and here she is!"

After that she forgot Ronicky Doone and the rest of the world except Gregg, as he took her in his arms and asked over and over: "How did it come about? How did it come about?"

And over and over she answered: "It was Ronicky, Bill. We owe everything to him and Ruth Tolliver."

This brought from Ronicky a sudden question: "And what of her? What of Ruth Tolliver? She wouldn't come?"

It pricked the bubble of Caroline's happiness, that question. Staring at the frowning face of Ronicky Doone her heart for a moment misgave her. How could she tell the truth? How could she admit her cowardice which had accepted Ruth's great sacrifice?

"No," she said at last, "Ruth stayed."

"Talk about that afterward, Ronicky," pleaded Bill Gregg. "I got about a million things to say to Caroline."

"I'm going to talk now," said Ronicky gravely. "They's something queer about the way Caroline said that. Will you let me ask you a few more questions?"

"Won't you wait?" asked Caroline, in an agony of remorse and shame. "Won't you wait till the morning?"

Ronicky Doone walked up and down the room

for a moment. He had no wish to break in upon the long delayed happiness of these two. While he paced he heard Bill Gregg saying that they must start at once and put three thousand miles between them and that devil, John Mark; and he heard Caroline say that there was no longer anything to fear—the claws of the devil had been trimmed, and he would not reach after them—he had promised. At that Ronicky whirled sharply on them again.

"What made Mark change his mind about you?" he asked. "He isn't the sort to change his mind without a pretty good reason. What bought him off? Nothing but a price would change him, I guess."

And she had to admit: "It was Ruth."

"She paid the price?" he asked harshly. "How, Caroline?"

"She promised to marry him, Ronicky."

The bitter truth was coming now, and she cringed as she spoke it. The tall body of Ronicky Doone was trembling with excitement.

"She made that promise so that you could go free, Caroline?"   ·

"No, no!" exclaimed Bill Gregg.

"It's true," said the girl. "We were about to leave together when John Mark stopped us."

"Ruth was coming with you?" asked Ronicky. "Yes."

"And when Mark stopped you she offered herself in exchange for your freedom?"

"Y-yes!"

Both she and bill Gregg looked apprehensively at the dark face of Ronicky Doone, where a storm was gathering.

But he restrained his anger with a mighty effort. "She was going to cut away from that life and start over—is that straight, Caroline?"

"Yes."

"Get the police, Ronicky," said Bill Gregg. "They sure can't hold no woman agin' her will in this country."

"Don't you see that it is her will?" asked Ronicky Doone darkly. "Ain't she made a bargain? Don't you think she's ready and willing to live up to it? She sure is, son, and she'll go the limit to do what she's said she'll do. You stay here—I'll go out and tackle the job."

"Then I go, too," said Bill Gregg stoutly. "You been through enough for me. Here's where I go as far as you go. I'm ready when you're ready, Ronicky."

It was so just an offer that even Caroline dared not cry out against it, but she sat with her hands clasped close together, her eyes begging Ronicky to let the offer go. Ronicky Doone nodded slowly.

"I hoped you'd say that, Bill," he said. "But I'll tell you what: you stay here for a while, and I'll trot down and take a look around and try to figure out what's to be done. Can't just walk up and rap at the front door of the house, you know. And I can't go in the way I went before. No doubt about that. I got to step light. So let me go out and look around, will you, Bill? Then I'll come back and tell you what I've decided."

Once in the street Ronicky looked dubiously across at the opposite house. He realized that more than an hour had passed since Caroline had left John Mark's house. What had happened to Ruth in that hour? The front of the house was lighted in two or three windows, but those lights could tell him nothing. From the inside of the house he could locate Ruth's room again, but from the outside it was impossible for him to do it.

The whole house, of course, was thoroughly guarded against his attack, for attack they knew he would. The only question was from what angle he would deliver his assault. In that case, of course, the correct thing was to find the unexpected means. But how could he outguess a band of trained criminals? They would have foreseen far greater subtleties than any he could attempt. They would be so keen that the best way to take them by surprise might be simply to step up to the house, ring the door bell and enter, if the door were opened.

The idea intrigued him at once. They might be, and no doubt were, guarding every obscure cellar window, every skylight. To trick them was impossible, but it was always possible to bluff any man—even John Mark and his followers.

Straight across the street marched Ronicky Doone and up the steps of the opposite house and rang the bell—not a timid ring, but two sharp pressures, such as would announce a man in a hurry, a brisk man who did not wish to be delayed.

He took only one precaution, pulling his hat down so that the black shadow of the brim would fall like a robber's mask across the upper part of his face. Then he waited, as a man both hurried and certain, turning a little away from the door, at an angle which still more effectually concealed him, while he tapped impatiently with one foot.

Presently the door opened, after he made certain that someone had looked out at him from the side window. How much had they seen? How much had they guessed as to the identity of this night visitor? The softness of the opening of the door and the whisper of the wind, as it rushed into the hall beyond, were like a hiss of threatening secrecy. And then, from the shadow of that meager opening a voice was saying: "Who's there?"

The very caution, however, reassured Ronicky Doone. Had they suspected that it was he they would either have kept the door definitely closed, or else they would have flung it open and boldly invited him in.

"I want to see Harry Morgan—quick!" he said and stepped close to the door.

At his bold approach the door was closed like the winking of an eye, until it was barely an inch ajar.

"Keep back!" came the warning through this small opening. "Keep clear, bo!"

"Damnation!" exclaimed Ronicky. "What's the idea? I want Harry, I tell you."

"Harry ain't here."

"Just hand me that piece of paper over there, and I'll write out the message," said Ronicky, pointing to the little table just beyond the doorman. The latter turned with a growl, and the moment he was halfway around Ronicky Doone sprang in. His right arm fastened around the head of the unlucky warder and, passing down to his throat, crushed it in a strangle hold. His other hand, darting out in strong precision, caught the right arm of the warder at the wrist and jerked it back between his shoulders. In an instant he was effectively gagged and bound by those two movements, and Ronicky Doone, pausing for an instant to make sure of himself, heard footsteps in the hall above.

It was too late to do what he had hoped, yet he must take his prize out of the way. For that purpose he half carried, half dragged his victim through the doorway and into the adjoining room. There he deposited him on the floor, as near death as life. Relaxing his hold on the man's throat, he whipped out his Colt and tucked the cold muzzle under the chin of the other.

"Now don't stir," he said; "don't whisper, don't move a muscle. Partner, I'm Ronicky Doone. Now talk quick. Where's Ruth Tolliver?"

"Upstairs."

"In her room?"

"Yes."

Ronicky started to rise, then, for there had been a slight fraction of a second's pause before the victim answered, he changed his mind. "I ought to smash your head open for that lie," he

Max Brand

said at a random guess. "Tell me straight, now, where's Ruth Tolliver?"

"How can I tell, if she ain't in her room?"

"Look," said Ronicky Doone, "if anyone comes into the hall before you've told me where the girl is, you're dead, partner. That's straight, now talk."

"She's with Mark."

"And where's he?"

"He'd kill me if I tell."

"Not if I find him before he finds you. His killing days are ended! Where's Mark and the girl? Has he run off with her?"

"Yes."

"They're married?" asked Ronicky, feeling that it might be a wild-goose chase after all."

"I dunno."

"But where are they?"

"Heaven help me, then! I'll tell you."

He began to whisper swiftly, incoherently, his voice shaking almost to silence, as he reached the heart of his narrative.

234

Chapter Twenty-six

Hills and Sea

The summerhouse lay in a valley between two hills; resting on the lawn before it Ruth Tolliver lay with her head pillowed back between her hands, and the broad brim of her straw that flopped down to shade her eyes. She could look up on either side to the sweep of grass, with the wind twinkling in it—grass that rolled smoothly up to the gentle blue sky beyond. On the one hand it was very near to her, that film of blue, but to her right the narrow, bright heads of a young poplar grove pushed up beyond the hilltop, and that made the sky fall back an immeasurable distance. Not very much variety in that landscape, but there was an infinite variety in the changes of the open-air silence. Overtones, all of them—but what a range!

If she found that what was immediately over-head and beside her was too bland, if she wearied of that lovely drift of clouds across the sky, then she had only to raise herself upon one elbow and look down to the broad, white band of the earth, and the startling blue of the ocean beyond. She was a little way up among the hills, to be sure, but, in spite of her elevation, when she looked out toward the horizon it seemed that the sea was hollowed like a great bowl—that the horizon wave was apt at any moment to roll in upon the beach and overwhelm her among the hills.

Not a very great excitement for such a girl as Ruth Tolliver, to be sure. Particularly when the faint crease between her eyes told of a perpetual worry and a strain under which she was now living. She was trying to lose herself in forget-fulness, in this open, drowsy climate.

Behind her a leisurely step came down one of the garden paths. It brought her to attention at once. A shadow passed across her face, and instantly she was sitting up, alert and excited.

John Mark sat down cross-legged beside her, a very changed John Mark, indeed. He wore white trousers and low white shoes, with a sack coat of blue—a cool-looking man even on this sultry day. The cane, which he insisted upon at all times, he had planted between his knees to help in the process of lowering himself to the ground. Now he hooked the head over his shoulder, pushed back his hat and smiled at the girl.

"Everything is finished," he said calmly. "How well you look, Ruth—that hair of yours against the green grass. Everything is finished; the license and the clergyman will arrive here within the hour."

She shrugged her shoulders. As a rule she tried at least to be politely acquiescent, but now and then something in her revolted. But John Mark was an artist in choosing remarks and moments which should not be noticed. Apparently her silence made not even a ripple on the calm surface of his assurance.

He had been so perfectly diplomatic, indeed, during the whole affair, that she had come to respect and fear him more than ever. Even in that sudden midnight departure from the house in Beekman Place, in that unaccountable panic which made him decide to flee from the vicinity of Ronicky Doone—even in that critical moment he had made sure that there was a proper chaperon with them. During all her years with him he had always taken meticulous care that she should be above the slightest breath of suspicion—a strange thing when the work to which he had assigned her was considered.

"Well," he asked, "now that you've seen, how do you like it? If you wish, we'll move today after the ceremony. It's only a temporary halting place, or it can be a more or less permanent home, just as you please."

It rather amused her to listen to this deprecatory manner of speech. Of course she could direct him in small matters, but in such a thing as the choice of a residence she knew that in the end he would absolutely have his own way.

"I don't know," she said. "I like silence just now. I'll stay here as long as you're contented."

He pressed her hand very lightly; it was the only time he had caressed her since they left New York, and his hand left hers instantly.

"Of course," he explained, "I'm glad to be at a distance for a time—a place to which we can't be followed."

"By Ronicky Doone?" Her question had sprung impulsively to her lips.

"Exactly." From the first he had been amazingly frank in confessing his fear of the Westerner. "Who else in the world would I care about for an instant? Where no other has ever crossed me once successfully, he has done so twice. That, you know, makes me begin to feel that my fate is wrapped up in the young devil."

He shuddered at the thought, as if a cold wind had struck him.

"I think you need not worry about him," said the girl faintly. "I suppose by this time he is in such a condition that he will never worry another soul in the world."

The other turned and looked at her for a long, grave moment.

"You think he attempted to break into the house?"

"And didn't you expect the same thing? Why else did you leave New York?"

"I confess that was my idea, but I think no harm has come to him. The chances are nine out of ten, at least, that he has not been badly hurt."

She turned away, her hands clenched hard.

"Oh my honor," he insisted with some emotion. "I gave directions that, if he made an attack, he was not to be harmed more than necessary to disarm him."

"Knowing that to disarm him would mean to kill him."

"Not at all. After all he is not such a terrible fellow as that—not at all, my dear. A blow, a shot might have dropped him. But, unless it were followed by a second, he would not be killed. Single shots and single blows rarely kill, you know."

She nodded more hopefully, and then her eyes turned with a wide question upon her companion.

He answered it at once with the utmost frankness.

"You wonder why I gave such orders when I dread Doone—when I so dread Doone—when I so heartily want him out of my way forever? I'll tell you. If Doone were killed there would be a shadow between us at once. Not that I believe you love him—no, that cannot be. He may have touched your heart, but he cannot have convinced your head, and you are equal parts of brain and soul, my dear. Therefore you cannot love him."

She controlled the faintest of smiles at the surety of his analysis. He could never escape from an old conclusion that the girl must be in large part his own product—he could never keep from attributing to her his own motives.

"But just suppose," she said, "that Ronicky Doone broke into your house, forced one of your men to tell him where we are, and then followed us at once. He would be about due to arrive now. What if all that happened?"

He smiled at her. "If all that happened, you are quite right; he would be about due to arrive. I suppose, being a Westerner, that the first thing he would do in the village would be to hire a horse to take him out here, and he would come galloping yonder, where you see that white road tossing over the hills."

"And what if he does come?" she asked.

"Then," said John Mark very gravely, "he will indeed be in serious danger. It will be the third time that he has threatened me. And the third time—"

"You've prepared even for his coming here?" she asked, the thought tightening the muscles of her throat.

"When you have such a man as Ronicky Doone on your hands," he confessed, "you have to be ready for anything. Yes, I have prepared. If he comes he'll come by the straightest route, certain that we don't expect him. He'll run blindly into the trap. Yonder—you see where the two hills almost close over the road—yonder is Shorty Kruger behind the rocks, waiting and watching. A very good gunman is Shorty. Know him?"

"Yes," she said, shuddering. "Of course I know him."

"But even suppose that the passes Kruger—down there in the hollow, where the road bends in toward us, you can see Lefty himself. I wired him to come, and there he is."

"Lefty?" asked the girl, aghast.

"Lefty himself," said John Mark. "You see how much I respect Ronicky Doone's fighting properties? Yes, Lefty himself, the great, the infallible Lefty!"

She turned her back on the white road which led from the village and faced the sea.

"If we are down here long enough," he said, "I'll have a little wharf built inside that cove. You see? Then we can bring up a motor boat and anchor it in there. Do you know much about boats?"

"Almost nothing."

"That's true, but we'll correct it. Between you and me, if I had to choose between a boat and a horse I don't know which I should—"

Two sharp detonations cut off his words. While he raised a startled hand for silence they remained staring at one another, and the long, faint echoes rolled across the hills.

"A revolver shot first, far off," he said, "and then a rifle shot. That metallic clang always means a rifle shot."

He turned, and she turned with him. Covering their eyes from the white light of the sun they peered at the distant road, where, as he had pointed out, the two hills leaned together and left a narrow footing between.

"The miracle has happened," said John Mark in a perfectly sober voice. "It is Ronicky Doone!"

Chapter Twenty-seven

The Last Stand

At the same instant she saw what his keener eye had discerned the moment before. A small trail of dust was blowing down the road, just below the place where the two hills leaned together. Under it was the dimly discernible, dust-veiled form of a horseman riding at full speed.

"Fate is against me," said John Mark in his quiet way. "Why should this dare-devil be destined to hunt me? I can gain nothing by his death but your hate. And, if he succeeds in breaking through Lefty, as he has broken through Kruger, even then he shall win nothing. I swear it!"

As he spoke he looked at her in gloomy resolution, but the girl was on fire—fear and joy were fighting in her face. In her ecstasy she was clinging to the man beside her.

"Think of it—think of it!" she exclaimed. "He has done what I said he would do. Ah, I read his mind! Ronicky Doone, Ronicky Doone, was there ever your like under the wide, wide sky? He's brushed Kruger out of his way—"

"Not entirely," said John Mark calmly, "not entirely, you see?"

As he spoke they heard again the unmistakable sound of a rifle shot, and then another and another, ringing from the place where the two hills leaned over the road.

"It's Kruger," declared John Mark calmly. "That chivalrous idiot, Doone, apparently shot him down and didn't wait to finish him. Very clever work on his part, but very sloppy. However, he seems to have wounded Kruger so badly that my gunman can't hit his mark."

For Ronicky Doone, if it were indeed he, was still galloping down the road, more and more clearly discernible, while the rifle firing behind him ceased.

"Of course that firing will be the alarm for Lefty," went on John Mark, seeming to enjoy the spectacle before him, as if it were a thing from which he was entirely detached. "And Lefty can make his choice. Kruger was his pal. If he wants to revenge the fall of Kruger he may shoot from behind a tree. If not, he'll shoot from the open, and it will be an even fight."

The terror of it all, the whole realization, sprang up in the girl. In a moment she was crying: "Stop him, John—for Heaven's sake, find a way to stop him."

"There is only one power that can turn the trick, I'm afraid," answered John Mark. "That power is Lefty."

"If he shoots Lefty he'll come straight toward us on his way to the house, and if he sees you—"

"If he sees me he'll shoot me, of course," declared Mark.

She stared at him. "John," she said, "I know you're brave, but you won't try to face him?"

"I'm fairly expert with a gun." He added: "But it's good of you to be concerned about me."

"I am concerned, more than concerned, John. A woman has premonitions, and I tell you I know, as well as I know I'm standing here, that if you face Ronicky Doone you'll go down."

"You're right," replied Mark. "I fear that I have been too much of a specialist, so I shall not face Doone."

"Then start for the house—and hurry!"

"Run away and leave you here?"

The dust cloud and the figure of the rider in it were sweeping rapidly down on the grove in the hollow, where Lefty waited. And the girl was torn between three emotions: Joy at the coming of the adventurer, fear for him, terror at the thought of his meeting with Mark.

"It would be murder, John! I'll go with you if you'll start now!"

"No," he said quietly, "I won't run. Besides it is impossible for him to take you from me."

"Impossible?" she asked. "What do you mean?"

"When the time comes you'll see! Now he's nearly there—watch!"

The rider was in full view now, driving his horse at a stretching gallop. There was no doubt about the identity of the man. They could not make out his face, of course, at that distance, but something in the careless dash of his seat in the saddle, something about the slender, erect body cried out almost in words that this was Ronicky Doone. A moment later the first treetops of the grove brushed across him, and he was lost from view.

The girl buried her face in her hands, then she looked up. By this time he must have reached Lefty, and yet there was no sound of shooting. Had Lefty found discretion the better part of valor and let him go by unhindered? But, in that case, the swift gallop of the horse would have borne the rider through the grove by this time.

"What's happened?" she asked of John Mark. "What can have happened down there?"

"A very simple story," said Mark. "Lefty, as I feared, has been more chivalrous than wise. He has stepped out into the road and ordered Ronicky to stop, and Ronicky has stopped. Now he is sitting in his saddle, looking down to Lefty, and they are holding a parley—very like two knights of the old days, exchanging compliments before they try to cut each other's throats."

But, even as he spoke, there was the sound of a gun exploding, and then a silence.

"One shot—one revolver shot," said John Mark in his deadly calm voice. "It is as I said. They drew at a signal, and one of them proved far the faster. It was a dead shot, for only one was needed to end the battle. One of them is standing, the other lies dead under the shadow of that grove, my dear. Which is it?"

"Which is it?" asked the girl in a whisper. Then she threw up her hands with a joyous cry: "Ronicky Doone! Ronicky, Ronicky Doone!"

A horseman was breaking into view through the grove, and now he rode out into full view below them—unmistakably Ronicky Doone! Even at that distance he heard the cry, and, throwing up his hand with a shout that tingled faintly up to them, he spurred straight up the slope toward them. Ruth Tolliver started forward, but a hand closed over her wrist with a biting grip and brought her to a sudden halt. She turned to find John Mark, an automatic hanging loosely in his other hand.

His calm had gone, and in his dead-white face the eyes were rolling and gleaming, and his set lips trembled. "You were right," he said, "I cannot face him. Not that I fear death, but there would be a thousand damnations in it if I died knowing that he would have you after my eyes were closed. I told you he could not take you—not living, my dear. Dead he may have us both."

"John!" said the girl, staring and bewildered. "In the name of pity, John, in the name of all the goodness you have showed me, don't do it."

He laughed wildly. "I am about to lose the one thing on earth I have ever cared for, and still I can smile. I am about to die by my own hand, and still I can smile. For the last time, will you stand up like your old brave self?"

"Mercy!" she cried. "In Heaven's name—"

"Then have it as you are!" he said, and she saw the sun flash on the steel, and he raised the gun.

She closed her eyes—waited—heard the distant drumming of hoofs on the turf of the hillside. Then she caught the report of a gun.

But it was strangely far away, that sound. She thought at first that the bullet must have numbed, as it struck her. Presently a shooting pain would pass through her body—then death.

Opening her bewildered eyes she beheld John Mark staggering, the automatic lying on the ground, his hands clutching at his breast. Then glancing to one side she saw the form of Ronicky Doone riding as fast as spur would urge his horse, the long Colt balanced in his hand. That, then, was the shot she had heard—a longe-range chance shot when he saw what was happening on top of the hill.

So swift was Doone's coming that, by the time she had reached her feet again, he was beside her, and they leaned over John Mark together. As they did so Mark's eyes opened, then they closed again, as if with pain. When he looked again his sight was clear.

"As I expected," he said dryly, "I see your faces together—both together, and actually wasting sympathy on me? Tush, tush! So rich in happiness that you can waste time on me?"

"John," said the girl on her knees and weeping beside him, "you know that I have always cared for you, but as a brother, John, and not—"

"Really," he said calmly, "you are wasting emotion. I am not going to die, and I wish you would put a bandage around me and send for some of the men at the house to carry me up there. That bullet of yours—by Harry, a very pretty snap shot—just raked across my breast, as far as I can make out. Perhaps it broke a bone or two, but that's all. Yes, I am to have the pleasure of living."

His smile was ghastly thing, and, growing suddenly weak, as if for the first time in his life he allowed his indomitable spirit to relax, his head fell to one side, and he lay in a limp faint.

Chapter Twenty-eight

Hope Deferred

Time in six months brought the year to the early spring, that time when even the mountain desert forgets its sternness for a month or two. Six months had not made Bill Gregg rich from his mine, but it had convinced him, on the contrary, that a man with a wife must have a sure income, even if it be a small one.

He squatted on a small piece of land, gathered a little herd, and, having thrown up a four-room shack, he and Caroline lived as happily as king and queen. Not that domains were very large, but, from their hut on the hill, they could look over a fine sweep of country, which did not all belong to them, to be sure, but which they constantly promised themselves should one day be theirs.

It was the dull period of the afternoon, the quiet, waiting period which comes between three or four o'clock and the sunset, and Bill and his wife sat in the shadow of the mighty silver spruce before their door. The great tree was really more of a home for them than the roof they had built to sleep under.

Presently Caroline stood up and pointed. "She's coming," she said, and, looking down the hillside, she smiled in anticipation.

The rider below them, winding up the trail, looked up and waved, then urged her horse to a full gallop for the short remnant of the distance before her. It was Ruth Tolliver who swung down from the saddle, laughing and joyous from the ride.

A strangely changed Ruth she was. She had turned to a brown beauty in the wind and the sun of the West, a more buoyant and more graceful beauty. She had accepted none of the offers of John Mark, but, leaving her old life entirely behind her, as Ronicky Doone had suggested, she went West to make her own living. With Caroline and Bill Gregg she had found a home, and her work was teaching the valley school, half a dozen miles away.

"Any mail?" asked Bill, for she passed the distant group of mail boxes on her way to the school.

At that the face of the girl darkened. "One letter," she said, "and I want you to read it aloud, Caroline. Then we'll all put our heads together and see if we can make out what it means." She handed the letter to Caroline, who shook it out. "It's from Ronicky," she exclaimed.

"It's from Ronicky," said Ruth Tolliver gravely, so gravely that the other two raised their heads and cast silent glances at her.

Caroline read aloud: "Dear Ruth, I figure that I'm overdue back at Bill's place by about a month—"

"By two months," corrected Ruth soberly.

"And I've got to apologize to them and you for being so late. Matter of fact I started right pronto to get back on time, but something turned up. You see, I went broke."

Caroline dropped the letter with an exclamation. "Do you think he's gone back to gambling, Ruth?"

"No," said the girl. "He gave me his promise never to play for money again, and a promise from Ronicky Doone is as good as minted gold."

"It sure is," agreed Bill Gregg.

Caroline went on with the letter: "I went broke because Pete Darnely was in a terrible hole, having fallen out with his old man, and Pete needed a lift. Which of course I gave him pronto, Pete being a fine gent."

There was an exclamation of impatience from Ruth Tolliver.

"Isn't that like Ronicky? Isn't that typical?"

"I'm afraid it is," said the other girl with a touch of sadness. "Dear old Ronicky, but such a wild man!"

She continued in the reading: "But I've got a scheme on now by which I'll sure get a stake and come back, and then you and me can get married, as soon as you feel like saying the word. The scheme is to find a lost mine—"

"A lost mine!" shouted Bill Gregg, his practical miner's mind revolting at this idea. "My guns, is Ronicky plumb nutty? That's all he's got to do—just find a 'lost mine?' Well, if that ain't plenty, may I never see a yearling ag'in!"

"Find a lost mine," went on Caroline, her voice trembling between tears and laughter, "and sink a new shaft, a couple of hundred feet to find where the old vein—"

"Sink a shaft a couple of hundred feet!" said Bill Gregg. "And him broke! Where'll he get the money to sink the shaft?"

"When we begin to take out the pay dirt," went on Caroline, "I'll either come or send for you and—"

"Hush up!" said Bill Gregg softly.

Caroline looked up and saw the tears streaming down the face of Ruth Tolliver. "I'm so sorry, poor dear!" she whispered, going to the other girl. But Ruth Tolliver shook her head.

"I'm only crying," she said, "because it's so delightfully and beautifully and terribly like Ronicky to write such a letter and tell of such plans. He's given away a lot of money to help some spendthrift, and now he's gone to get more money by finding a 'lost mine!' But do you see what it means, Caroline? It means that he doesn't love me—really!"

"Don't love you?" asked Bill Gregg. "Then he's a plumb fool. Why—"

"Hush, Bill," put in Caroline. "You mustn't say that," she added to Ruth. "Of course you have reason to be sad about it and angry, too."

"Sad, perhaps, but not angry," said Ruth Tolliver. "How could I ever be really angry with Ronicky? Hasn't he given me a chance to live a clean life? Hasn't he given me this big free open West to live in? And what would I be without Ronicky? What would have happened to me in New York? Oh, no, not angry. But I've simply waked up, Caroline. I see now that Ronicky never cared particularly about me. He was simply in love with the danger of my position. As a matter of fact I don't think he ever told me in so many words that he loved me. I simply took it for granted because he did such things for me as even a man in love would not have done. After the danger and uniqueness were gone Ronicky simply lost interest."

"Don't say such things!" exclaimed Caroline.

"It's true," said Ruth steadily. "If he really wanted to come here—well, did you ever hear of anything Ronicky wanted that he didn't get?"

"Except money," suggested Bill Gregg. "Well, he even gets that, but most generally he gives it away pretty pronto."

"He'd come like a bullet from a gun if he really wanted me," said Ruth. "No, the only way I can bring Ronicky is to surround myself with new dangers, terrible dangers, make myself a lost cause again. Then Ronicky would come laughing and singing, eager as ever. Oh, I think I know him!"

"And what are you going to do?" asked Caroline.

"The only thing I can do," said the other girl. "I'm going to wait."

Far, far north two horsemen came at that same moment to a splitting of the trail they rode. The elder, bearded man, pointed ahead.

"That's the roundabout way," he said, "but it's sure the only safe way. We'll travel there, Ronicky, eh?"

Ronicky Doone lifted his head, and his bay mare lifted her head at the same instant. The two were strangely in touch with one another.

"I dunno," he said, "I ain't heard of anybody taking the short cut for years—not since the big slide in the canyon. But I got a feeling I'd sort of like to try it. Save a lot of time and give us a lot of fun."

"Unless it breaks our necks."

"Sure," said Ronicky, "but you don't enjoy having your neck safe and sound, unless you take a chance of breaking it, once in a while."

Max Brand is the best-known pen name of Frederick Faust, creator of Dr. Kildare, Destry, and many other fictional characters popular with readers and viewers worldwide. Faust wrote for a variety of audiences in many genres. His enormous output, totaling approximately thirty million words or the equivalent of 530 ordinary books, covered nearly every field: crime, fantasy, historical romance, espionage, Westerns, science fiction, adventure, animal stories, love, war, and fashionable society, big business and big medicine. Eighty motion pictures have been based on his work along with many radio and television programs. For good measure he also published four volumes of poetry. Perhaps no other author has reached more people in more different ways.

Born in Seattle in 1892, orphaned early, Faust grew up in the rural San Joaquin Valley of California. At Berkeley he became a student rebel and one-man literary movement, contributing prodigiously to all campus publications. Denied a degree because of unconventional conduct, he embarked on a series of adventures culminating in New York City where, after a period of near starvation, he received simultaneous recognition as a serious poet and successful popular-prose writer. Later, he traveled widely, making his home in New York, then in Florence, and finally in Los Angeles.

Once the United States entered the Second World War, Faust abandoned his lucrative writing career and his work as a screenwriter to serve as a war correspondent with the infantry in Italy, despite his fifty-one years and a bad heart. He was killed during a night attack on a hilltop village held by the German army. New books based on magazine serials or unpublished manuscripts continue to appear. Alive and dead he has averaged a new one every four months for seventy-five years. In the U.S. alone nine publishers issue his work, plus many more in foreign countries. Yet, only recently have the full dimensions of this extraordinarily versatile and prolific writer come to be recognized and his stature as a protean literary figure in the 20th Century acknowledged. His popularity continues to grow throughout the world.